walking in the rain

CHERYL BURMAN

This is a work of fiction. Names, characters, businesses, places, events, locales, and incidents are either the products of the author's imagination or used in a fictitious manner. Any resemblance to actual persons, living or dead, or actual events is purely coincidental.

First published in the UK in 2023 by Holborn House Ltd

©2023 Cheryl Burman

Apart from any use permitted under UK copyright law, this publication may only be reproduced, stored, or transmitted, in any form, or by any means, with the prior permission in writing of the publishers or, in the case of reprographic production, in accordance with the terms and licences issued by the Copyright Licensing Agency.

By Cheryl Burman

Keepers

Sequel

Walking in the Rain

River Witch

SHORT STORIES

Dragon Gift

GUARDIANS OF THE FOREST TRILOGY

The Wild Army

Quests

Gryphon Magic

Prequel

Legend of the Winged Lion

www.cherylburman.com

Foreword

The final scenes of *Keepers* are set in the Australian Snowy Mountains early in the days of the gargantuan Snowy Mountains Hydro-Electric Scheme. The Scheme also provides the backdrop to much of *Walking in the Rain*. While I have given brief explanations where they would occur naturally, some readers might like to know more about this amazing engineering feat which took some twenty-five years to construct and turned rivers around, all to provide water to Australia's dry hinterland. Read about it on my website at https://cherylburman.com/snowy-mountains-scheme/.

Chapter One

Winter 1954

June steps gingerly from wet patch to wet patch where the footpath has been imperfectly swept of snow. Her toes curl in on themselves inside her boots, preserving their remaining warmth. Having lived all her life in the Australian alps, the bitter winds and snow-piled streets and roofs of her home town of Cooma are merely signs of unwelcome weather. Snow can be a picturesque treat when the sun shines and warms the old stone buildings above their verandahed facades. Today, however, louring clouds hang above the town, obscuring the view of the Snowy Mountains dominating the end of the main street. Anyway, June is in a hurry with no time for views, or the inclination to admire them. Her mind buzzes from last night's conversation. A bemused buzzing.

She turns into a residential street where a row of snow gums live up to their name. The wind buffets her tightly closed coat, and she clutches her woollen hat to save it being whipped from her head. A gloomy dawn lightens the rest of her short journey to the hospital, where she follows the passage to the nurses' staff room. When she pushes open the door, she whooshes out a breath of gratitude for the warm stuffiness.

Two night shift nurses sit at a long table, cups before them. The air is redolent with scents of hot cocoa and cigarettes, tinged with a hint of sweaty nurse.

'Morning, Libby, morning Stella.' June pulls off her hat and hangs it on one of a row of hooks on the wall.

'Morning, June.' They are loud, cheerful, off for twelve hours to sleep, eat and make merry. If they can in this godawful weather.

'Hope neither of you is expecting to go far today.' June wriggles out of her coat, which joins the hat. She smooths her blonde curls and pats her uniform before sitting on a long bench beneath the hooks to exchange her boots for nurse's shoes.

A gleeful, shouted 'No kidding!' accompany her tying of white laces. She wriggles her toes, encouraging circulation. She'll have a cup of tea, a piece of toast, before starting her shift.

'Well …?' Libby swings about in her seat to give June an arch stare. 'Did you see Peter last night?'

June's head jerks up. Is Libby reading her mind? No, of course not. Teasing in her normal way.

'I did.' June finishes tying her laces, stands and heads to the kettle.

'Well …?' Libby pushes her palms together and widens her eyes in mock excitement.

'I had dinner there. With Peter.' She pauses, briefly. 'And his children.' June adds the last bit before Libby can extrapolate activities in her over-active mind.

'And …?'

'And nothing.' She jiggles the kettle to check the water level. 'Can I have my cup of tea in peace, please?' It comes out more tartly than she means, because the kettle jiggling brings the confused buzzing into clear focus.

It was a cup of tea that caused the frostiness last night. June pulls in her lips. A stupid hot drink. Whether she had time to stay for one (and make it, naturally) before heading home. She hadn't, not when she pulled the heavy curtains in Peter's house an inch apart to reveal a darkness faintly lit by falling white stuff coating the new neighbourhood's red roof tiles. She had let the curtain fall closed.

'I don't want to drive in this, I'm heading off.'

'Stay here, stay with me tonight.'

'No.' The subtle demand in his tone forced a faked lightness in hers. 'The kids asked awkward questions last time.'

The kids, aged five and seven, had said, 'Are you going to be our new mummy?'

June hadn't been sure whether they approved the idea or not, and there's been no enlightenment given her studious avoidance of being in Peter's house when the kids wake.

In any case, the kids have a mummy. Somewhere out there.

'Disappointing date?' It's Stella who asks, her question kind.

For a heartbeat, June is confused, thinking Stella is commenting on June's unspoken thought about the kids' mother.

'No, it's all good.' June tops up the kettle, places it on a gas ring and moves the conversation to a more professional level. 'Any problems?'

'Nothing came in.' Stella brings her cup and saucer to the sink. 'New mum in maternity is struggling with feeding, might need sympathy and help.' She turns the hot water tap, sending the wall-mounted heater into a hissing bout of hard work.

'No ambulances?'

'No, all quiet, thank goodness.' Libby takes up a tea towel. 'Don't expect it to last, not with all this snow.' She grins. 'You'll have a nice array of broken legs, hips and wrists to deal with, June.'

'I'll look forward to it.' She does, because a busy shift means no time to think. Specifically, to think about Peter's disappointed tut, his farewell as cool as the night air she had stepped into. To think about where this is going. If anywhere.

◇◇◇◇◇

Libby proves prescient. The shift is busy and June, her fellow nurses, and the doctor deal with a variety of non-deadly emergencies throughout the morning. A woman is brought in with a sprained wrist from a fall. An elderly man is rescued from his unheated home and warmed up while relatives are found to take him in. A scheduled tonsillectomy is cancelled because the child's parents can't get him to the hospital. The wind abandons its blustering showiness, and snow drifts from steel grey skies, languorous, in no hurry to move on.

During a break, June lifts her coat over her shoulders and walks the wide verandah, taking five minutes for herself. Banks of snow pile at the edges, overspilling onto the century-old wooden boards. The garden is an undulating blanket, as white as any sheet on a hospital bed. She mentally goes over her next tasks, not wanting her thoughts to wander back to last night.

She's returning to the wards when an ambulance makes a cautious manoeuvre into the driveway, adding to the crisscross of wavering track marks. A memory bursts into June's mind. It could be the combination of ambulance and snow. Or maybe it's her recent encounter with the man she bumped into in the timber yard when she was delivering an order on Peter's behalf. She and the man stared like they should recognise each other and June got there first. It was Arthur, the friend of the trio who'd arrived at the hospital in a flurry of commotion one sleety night three years ago. They chatted briefly, she asked after the three – Teddy and Raine, and Alf.

Whatever it is, the scene in front of her brings unbidden, sharp memories of those few intense days.

Meeting the ambulance in the dead of night, watching the two unconscious men carried inside. The doctor helping the pregnant Raine out of his car, having followed the ambulance from Jindabyne, forty miles away. Her pale, strained face. And Alf, whom June had assumed was the husband, not least by his caring attentiveness. Turned out he wasn't. The husband was one of the injured whom the ambulance had brought in, and was possibly at death's door.

And the day of the baby's birth, how June came across the gentle Alf in the doorway of the maternity ward, one foot sliding across the squeaky linoleum, hands in pockets, eyes intent on the scene ahead. Raine leaning forward, holding the baby out to Teddy in his wheelchair. A repentant Teddy hesitant, watching Raine rather than the baby, as if asking permission, and Raine granting it, urging him to embrace their tiny daughter.

June thinks of Peter's coolness last night, the implication of not liking to be thwarted. And over such a silly thing compared to the drama then. She recalls the pain in Alf's eyes as he watched the young family. Understanding his role was done.

The scene has haunted her ever since.

Huddled in her coat, June watches the vehicle's hesitant braking to a stop, the driver and crew jumping out, striding around to open the doors. She will be needed. She pushes Alf's pain into the secret recess where it lives, a silent grief she can do nothing about, and hurries inside.

◇◇◇◇◇

The busy shift is over, the highlights being two broken legs, a sprained wrist, and bruised ribs sustained when the owner of the ribs' car careened into a telegraph pole. Plus the normal day-to-day happenings of a suspected heart attack, which turned out not to be the case, and two births, both boys. The new mum from last night is smugly feeding her newborn with grateful thanks to June for her patient encouragement.

The skies are grey with an occasional feathery flake settling on June's shoulders as she makes her way home. She stops by a grocer on Sharp Street for bread, milk and eggs. Omelette for dinner, a book, listen to music on the wireless, and an early night. A few underthings need rinsing, and she hopes they'll dry before she runs out of clean bras and panties. Passing Mrs Elbra's ladies and children's wear shop, she pauses outside, trying to decide if it would be easier to buy more.

A rainbow-coloured, frilled child's net petticoat takes centre place in the cluttered window display. June bites her top lip, considering. Peter's girl would adore it. Perhaps …

No, she can't be the giver. It's a gift a mother, an aunt or grandmother would buy for the special little girl in their life. Too personal, too soon.

Chapter Two

ALF NESTLES THE FINAL SCREWDRIVER in place and secures the flaps of the bag holding his electrician's tools. Scooping up his leather jacket from the bare wooden boards, he slides his arms into the sleeves and peers into the darkening rain from the doorway of the empty house. A zigzag of unfinished walls, concrete foundations marked by wooden pegs and string, stacks of multi-coloured bricks and roof tiles, litter a shadowed moonscape that has vanquished the green paddocks of yesteryear. Progress.

He pulls his leather helmet over his head and tugs on his gloves before hefting the tool bag over his shoulder. He turns to the grey-haired man stowing saws in a carpenter's case at the end of the room.

'G'night, Mr G.'

Mr Greene looks up, lifts his carpenter's pencil from behind his ear to point it at Alf. 'Night, Alf. Watch it on the road, awful slippy out there.'

'Yeah, I will. See you tomorrow.'

'You at Raine and Teddy's tonight?'

'Yeah.'

'Have a good time. Give the kids a hug from their old grandpa for me.'

Assuring the doting granddad he will, Alf glances at his watch. There's time to shower and change before heading off for dinner at Raine and Teddy's. His weekly visit, playing with the kids, sinking a beer with Teddy, chatting with Raine over the washing up while Teddy puts the littlies to bed. They are Alf's moments of domesticity, meant to carry him through the week before another recharge, on the assumption he needs it.

He calls a second 'Good night', zips and buckles his jacket and walks out into the embrace of the wet winter dusk. The bucketing rain – quietened to an insistent drizzle – has left the unmade roads on the half-built estate greasy as spilled oil. Wet clay and motorbikes aren't a good match in Alf's experience.

Glutinous mud churns under the bike's tyres, spraying Alf's legs. Through his goggles, he squints along the single beam of headlight creating a glistening veil above the poorly lit, rutted road. He slides past the last of the partly built houses, skids around a corner, and accelerates away from the bleak landscape of the new estate.

◇◇◇◇◇

When Alf arrives at Teddy's, he hangs his wet coat and helmet on an overflowing stand before following his host along a freezing hallway to a high-ceilinged, dilapidated lounge. A familiar figure hovers over the dubious warmth of a kerosene heater.

Alf lets out a cheerful hoot. 'Arthur! Great surprise!'

He pumps his old friend's hand, admiring Arthur's winter beard. Good for keeping warm up there in the mountains, Arthur says. It also suits his muscular frame, built over years of hard, physical work.

Teddy waves a beer and gestures at the sideboard where more beers are lined up in a straggling row.

Alf levers off a bottle cap while questioning Arthur. 'Paying us a flying visit, or have you finally come to your senses and decided drilling giant tunnels through the Snowy Mountains is a mug's game, and you're home for good?'

'Sadly, no.' Arthur's wide grin, at odds with his statement, makes Alf want to ask what's going on that could be so cheery. He frowns and shifts the topic elsewhere. 'Does this mean Maggie's here too?'

Alf hasn't seen Maggie recently. Unsurprising given her nurse's shift work.

'She's here.' Teddy gestures at the hall door. 'Reading her nephew *The Poky Little Puppy*. Keeps 'em both quiet.' He winks.

'You, Alf? How's life?' Arthur's grin softens, as if Alf's life is something to be worried about. Perhaps it is.

Walking in the Rain

Alf slumps to the sagging sofa with his beer, pushing aside books and toys. He raises his drink to his friends. 'All fine, busy. Tons of work with all this house building the government's pushing on with like there's no tomorrow.'

Arthur snorts. 'It's all these Pommy immigrants, they keep on coming, also like there's no tomorrow.'

Teddy matches the snort. He plucks a golden-furred teddy bear from an upholstered chair and falls into the cushions.

'Teddy says' – he gives the toy a sombre shake –' we were bloody clever to leave bombed-out, rationed-out London town when we did. And our former countrymen are waking up to the same.' He tucks the toy to his side. 'You've a job for life, Alf.'

Alf grunts. 'Yeah. Me, and your dad too. The lucky ones.'

A tingling in his neck tells Alf he's being watched. Raine stands in the doorway, tea towel over her shoulder, gazing at him.

She smiles a greeting. 'Teddy.' She turns to her husband. 'Go and say good night to Stevie. I've just been, checked on Jenny too. And tell Maggie to finish up whatever she's reading to him before this casserole dries up. Beef isn't cheap.' She flourishes the tea towel, bows. 'Dinner is served, gentlemen. Using the dining room tonight, big occasion I believe, so please make your way there.' And retreats into the enticing smells.

◇◇◇◇◇

The beef casserole is tender and peppery, and Alf savours every mouthful. The conversation is bright, full of teasing, and Maggie's ebullience exceeds its normal levels. Must be having Arthur home.

Alf pats his stomach. 'Great meal, Raine.'

Thanks are murmured all around the big table which is Raine's pride and joy. She bought it in a second-hand shop and – Alf has heard her tell many people – is waiting for Teddy to repair its watermarked, scratched surface, resurrect its French polish sheen.

Raine takes the praise graciously and turns to Maggie. 'Time?'

Maggie looks at Arthur. 'Time?' Her eyes are bright with whatever excitement is brewing.

Alf glances between the two.

Arthur coughs, taps his dessert spoon on the edge of his plate. 'Announcement to make.'

Ah. Alf has a clue where this is going. He smiles, anticipating.

Maggie taps Arthur's shoulder. 'Stand up,' and he scrambles out of his chair at the hissed command.

Alf's smile widens. Raine is smug. Teddy frowns.

Arthur coughs, more vigorously. 'Me and Maggie have an announcement to make.'

'About bloody time.' Teddy reaches for his beer. He's smiling too.

Maggie leans across Arthur to slap her brother's arm. 'You have no idea what the announcement is. Shut up and listen.'

Teddy rolls his eyes.

'We've set a date for the wedding.' Arthur looks at Maggie, and the love in his eyes brings a lump to Alf's throat.

Alf bangs his fist on the table. 'Yay, at last!'

'Next autumn, about April, May.' Maggie is quick to fill in the detail.

'Hardly a date.' Teddy emphasises his grumble by pointing his dirty knife at Raine. 'You knew and didn't bother to tell?'

Raine shrugs. 'You weren't the one had to make the special meal, or the chocolate pudding.'

'Has to be after my contract with the Hydro Scheme runs out in March.' Arthur gives Maggie the soft-eyed look. 'We've waited long enough, and by March we'll have the money for a very healthy deposit on a house, like we promised ourselves.'

Walking in the Rain

Maggie humphs. 'Like *you* promised yourself. We could have been married long ago if —'

Arthur collapses into his chair and draws her close, kissing her cheek to cut off her sentence. 'It'll be worth it, you'll see.'

Maggie huffs, resigned.

'Do you want a brand new house?' Alf has more than a passing interest in this, given he might help build Arthur and Maggie's home. He likes the idea, a sort of wedding present from himself.

'Absolutely!' Maggie leaves no doubt. 'Don't care where, so long as it's not too far from town for me to get to work.' She lifts her chin. 'I'm going to learn to drive. It'll be better than relying on buses for shift work.'

Alf has a vision of Maggie driving, taking the roads by storm as she takes everything else, and wonders if he might give up his bike and ride on those discarded buses.

'And after all those years building things up in the mountains —' Arthur gazes slowly around the shabby room '— don't think I want to take on this kind of work.'

Alf's lips twitch and he joins his friend's examination of the fancy, leak-damaged cornices separating a flaky ceiling from high walls scarred by curling, ochre-coloured wallpaper. Likely it looked good when it first went up thirty years ago to cover the seventy-year-old walls. A huge, threadbare rug partially covers the dark floorboards. Even with the rug and the possibly original, also threadbare, velvet curtains, a chill pervades the room. Alf will be glad to return to the equally faded glory of the lounge, where the kerosene heater might have warmed the edges of the cold.

Maggie joins the wall-gazers. 'When *are* you going to make a start on this place, Teddy?'

Raine glowers at Teddy and pinches her lips together.

'Yeah.' Alf adds to the assault. 'What's the plan? I mean, it's not like you don't have people to help you.'

Raine's scowl softens. 'Think of all the work you and

your dad, and Alf, put into the old cabin.' She sighs heavily. 'Sometimes I wish we'd stayed up there in the hills, with the kookaburra and the chickens, my veg garden.'

Alf gives Teddy a sideways look. 'And the woodshed with its fancy hammerbeam roof.'

Teddy ignores Alf's comment, tilts back his chair. 'No rush. I mean, we only bought it in February.'

Raine humphs. 'When it was 100 outside in the shade and we thought we were pretty clever buying a place which kept cool, and cheap too.'

'House might have been cheap. Doing it up costs money.' Teddy flicks his wrist. 'Gotta wait for the shop to take off.'

'And when will that be?' Maggie throws her hands out. 'Think I haven't worked out why Dad's doing plain old house carpentry these days? Huh? He doesn't mind it as much as you do, little brother, but you can't expect him to keep working to subsidise your business.'

'Our business.' Teddy's eyes snap. 'We're partners. It's up to both of us –'

'Come on!' Maggie stares in disbelief. '*You* need to be making a go of it –'

'I *am* making a go of it.' Teddy thumps his chair forward.

Alf jumps at the thud, which is immediately followed by Raine's sharp intervention.

'Stop it, you two. You'll wake the kids.' She stands. 'Let's go back into the warmth, we can eat sweets in there. I'll bring it in a moment.' Stacking plates, she throws first Teddy and then Maggie warning glares and carries on clearing up.

Maggie chuckles, her frivolous self restored. 'Sorry all. It's just, well, Dad seems more tired than usual at the end of a day, and I worry.'

'It's the nurse in you.' Arthur wraps a well-muscled arm around Maggie's shoulders. 'Strong as an ox, your dad. You imagine things because of your work.'

Maggie strokes his arm. 'I guess I do, love, thanks.' A pause, the click of cutlery on china. 'Brrr, it's cold in here. You guys go and warm up. I'll help Raine with this chocolate pudding.'

◇◇◇◇◇

Alf settles in a chair in need of re-upholstering, refusing Teddy's offer of another beer.

Arthur accepts and waves the bottle in the air. 'Guess who I saw in Cooma on my way home?'

'No clue.' Not strictly true, as Alf's thoughts spring immediately – why? – to the one person he knows, or once knew, in the Snowy Mountains town. It must be –

'Nurse June, remember her?' Arthur confirms Alf's idea. 'You told me how kind she was over all the excitement when Jenny was born early, Alf. I met her when I came to help out. Remember?'

'When I nearly died, you mean?' Teddy gulps his beer, straight-faced. 'Pushed off a mountain by a bloody frontloader.'

'Yeah, Teddy.' Alf's mind hovers over the memories of those dreadful – for many reasons – few days.

Teddy could have died, true, and not from the accident high in the snow-covered mountains. Raine had been ready to kill him for his stupid suspicions about Alf and Raine being lovers. Time has merely softened Alf's own murderous inclinations that Teddy could think so badly of his wife. There are reasons why those days haven't come up a lot in conversation over the last years.

He focuses on the factual events. 'Frights all round between you and Raine, and Jenny coming early. Nurse June helped, a lot.'

Friendly blue eyes, calm, sympathetic. And the help June gave wasn't restricted to the hospital. Alf lets himself dwell on the times he was persuaded to leave Raine or Teddy's bedside, and June showed him the sights, talking, listening. He stops the memories there, but curiosity prompts him.

'How'd you bump into her, Arthur?'

Arthur takes a mouthful of beer and swallows it before

answering. 'Had to order timber from a yard and she happened to be there. Guess she was ordering stuff too.'

'Ah. Did she look well?' Alf kids himself he's making polite conversation, enquiring after a pleasant, passing acquaintance.

Arthur slides him a look. 'Guess so. Asked about Raine and Jenny, and if Teddy was behaving himself.' He casts his eyes to the ceiling. 'I told her not bloody likely, which made her laugh.'

Teddy growls and says of course he's behaving. Family, work, running his own shop – he doesn't have a lot of choice.

Alf wants to ask if June mentioned him. He hesitates. It'll lead to mockery and questions.

'She asked about you too, Alf, whether you were okay.'

Alf raises his eyebrows. 'Okay?'

Arthur shrugs. 'Yeah. Whether you were okay.'

'And?' What other 'and' is he expecting?

'I said you were fine, same as ever, good old Alf.' He squints at Alf. 'Is there a hidden meaning behind that?'

'Nah.'

'Tell you what.' Arthur draws himself up tall, grin as wide as a laughing clown. 'Why don't you come back with me this time, find out for yourself? I mean, it's not like there's anything tying you here, right?'

No there isn't. Trust Arthur to utter the brutal truth. Alf twists about to face the kitchen. 'You think sweets'll be here soon, or will the whole wedding be planned first?'

◇◇◇◇◇

Arthur and Maggie leave straight after the pudding, and Alf helps Raine carry the bowls and spoons to the sink while Teddy deals with a fractious, wakeful Stevie.

Raine grimaces at the streaked plates and soaking casserole dish. 'Think I'll deal with it tomorrow. Don't have to work on a Saturday.'

'I'll help, get it over and done with.' Alf grabs a tea towel.

'Be a good chance for a chat. Like, what's going on with Teddy and the shop?'

Raine runs hot water to the accompaniment of gurgling, rattling pipes. 'One day it'll come flooding out.' She glances sideways at Alf. 'Teddy and the shop?'

'Yeah. I thought it was going well, stacks of work.'

'There *is* stacks of work. Problem is, Teddy's such a perfectionist it takes him an age to finish anything.' She pours detergent into the water, swishes it through with a cloth. 'Which means the cash coming in is spread over too long, which means to keep the place afloat, Mr Greene works on housing sites instead of helping Teddy with the basics, which means it takes even longer … See the problem?'

Alf sees. It doesn't surprise him. Teddy is no businessman.

'You and Faye doing okay, aren't you?'

'Yes.' Raine plunges a glass into the sink, swirls water through it and sets it on the rack. 'There's plenty of demand for temp secretaries and the like. There's enough business to pay the mortgage and feed us, barely. And Faye's helping by not taking her share while she's in Italy. A kind, sisterly gesture.' She screws up her nose. 'Thank God the mums are around to care for the kids, couldn't afford nursery care.'

'The grandmums love it, I bet. Hardly a burden with two of them to take it in turns.'

'I guess.'

Raine falls silent, whisking cutlery in and out of the foaming water.

'You guess?'

She gives him another frowning glance. 'It's Mrs Greene …'

'Again?' Alf polishes a glass, holds it to the dim bulb in a useless attempt to spot smears, and places it in a cupboard. 'I thought she was all good now, about you and Teddy. Loves the kids and all that.'

'Oh, no questioning her love for the kids. It's me she'll never accept, too much has happened.' Hands in the water,

Raine turns fully to Alf. 'This never goes further, right?'

He nods. What the hell?

'She nags me to give up working, says Faye can do it when she's finished swanning around Italy. Says that as Faye and Charlie apparently have no intention of having children, she should run the business and I should stay at home like a –' she screws up her nose and rolls her eyes '– real wife and mother.'

'Hmm.' Alf is unsurprised. He's known Teddy's mum all his life. She has strong views on everything there is to have views on. 'You love doing what you do.'

'Doesn't matter if I love it or not.' Raine's voice is matter of fact. 'No choice. It's what's keeping the wolf from the door.' She huffs softly. 'Sorry to put all this on you, Alf. You're too good a listener and – '

He gives her a small smile. 'I've always looked out for you, haven't I, Raine?'

A faint colour runs up Raine's neck. She laughs.

◇◇◇◇◇

Frosty stars shine white above the warm yellow of the streetlamps as Alf rides home. He parks, chains the bike at the back of the house and lets himself into his ground-floor flat.

He pulls down the roller blinds, tugs shut the sun-bleached curtains and reminds himself, for the umpteenth time, how new curtains are within his budget should he ever be motivated to buy them. Why improve the place for his landlord? Covering the brown linoleum with a rug he could take with him when/if he moved would make the place cosier, add a hint of warmth. Cosy for whom? Alf doesn't have many visitors.

He switches on the ancient electric heater, waiting for the wire elements to glow their tepid orange before going into the standing-room-for-one kitchenette where whiffs of breakfast's bacon greet him. Beer or tea, or cocoa to warm him up? He settles on a beer and sips from the bottle

Walking in the Rain

as he flips through his Johnny Ray records.

The black disc circles the turntable covering half the varnish-cracked sideboard, the words of "Just Walking in the Rain" drifting through Alf's mind as he sits with his head against the shabby sofa, eyes closed.

'Torturing my heart, trying to forget …'

The reality is that Alf has stopped torturing his heart. A tinge of sadness remains, as it will forever, he supposes. Things have changed, as the song reminds him, and his chance to win Raine for himself has gone, if it was ever realistic.

Teddy is a lucky man, as Alf frequently reminds his friend. They are good together, Teddy and Raine. She keeps his volatile moods at an even keel, doesn't put up with any self-centred nonsense. Although, this trouble over the cabinet-making business has Alf worried. He can't help it. Whatever happened in the past, Alf remains Raine's self-appointed watch dog.

The needle's hushed crackle breaks his chain of thought. He stretches, rescues the vinyl and places it carefully in its sleeve and into its slot on the shelf. He plays a second and a third, swapping the beer for a mug of cocoa, until the night turns late and it's well past time for bed. He should be fresh for tomorrow … a tomorrow that will be more of the same.

Chapter Three

FOR ARTHUR'S LAST NIGHT BEFORE heading back to the mountains, Raine and Teddy leave the kids with Raine's mother, and the five of them meet in the city to see *The Glenn Miller Story* and eat out.

The rain has hung about all week, gusting with a chilly southerly straight off Antarctica, as Raine says while they wait in the ticket queue.

Alf frowns at the tightness around her eyes. 'You okay?'

'Sure, why?'

'You look peaky.'

'Peaky? Tired is all, long hours at work plus sorting Teddy's accounts, and Jenny throwing two-year-old tantrums for the hell of it.' She rummages in her handbag for her purse. 'Life, Alfie, life.'

Afterwards, walking from the movie to the restaurant, Teddy is quiet, for him, and doesn't say much during the meal either. Likely those accounts are on his mind.

'Alf.' Arthur pats his stomach post a hearty serving of Baked Alaska. 'I've been thinking –'

'Dangerous.' Teddy's mutter comes with a quick lift of his eyebrows.

Arthur carries on. 'I've been thinking about what I said the other evening, and I reckon it'd be good for you to come up to the mountains. You need a change. Needn't be forever.'

'Catch up with Nurse June, hey?' Teddy comes to life at the chance to tease his friend. 'I liked Nurse June, and seems she remembers you, Alfie.'

'Nurse June?' Raine frowns. 'What's this about her? Why has she come up?' She casts a thoughtful glance at Alf, who shrugs.

'Arthur bumped into her in Cooma and she asked after us all.' He's abrupt. He doesn't want this conversation, it raises emotions he's played down for years. Also, they'll be piling in on him soon, telling him he needs to find a nice girl and what's wrong with the three or four Maggie has set him up with in the past. Nothing is wrong with them. They hadn't clicked, is all.

'I hear she asked specially after you, Alfie.' Maggie's eyes glitter and her red lipsticked mouth forms itself into a ludicrously lascivious leer.

Alf splutters his coffee. 'Not a good look, Maggie.' He pulls his face into mock-serious lines. 'You have to agree I was the one sane person at the time, apart from Jenny, so it makes perfect sense she liked me better than Raine and Teddy.'

Even Teddy finds this funny.

Arthur hasn't finished. 'I'm not joking, mate. You should think about it.'

'Yeah, I will.' In an abstract, what if, way. And then forget it again, or try to. He makes excuses for delay. 'Depths of winter not the best time to be heading up there.'

Raine mock shivers. 'Freezing, and since you lost all that weight you'll feel it more.'

Alf wraps his arms about himself and shivers in imitation, grateful to Raine for rescuing him.

◇◇◇◇◇

When Alf arrives at work a few mornings later, Mr Greene isn't hammering and sawing, ready for his first cup of tea. Alf lets himself in to the unfinished house, glad of the window glass puttied in place the day before to restrain the frigid wind. He sorts his screwdrivers and pliers with fingers icy from the ride. Mrs G must have one of her headaches and Mr G has been sent to the chemist for aspirin. He'll be along shortly.

The morning moves on. The plumbers arrive with kit for the bathroom and their loud chatter and clanking serve as a backdrop to Alf's own chattering thoughts. Past eleven, and no Mr G. Where is he? Has something happened?

By mid-afternoon, Alf has finished what he can for

today. He'll return later for the final fix, once the kitchen is in and the painting done. There's time left to start elsewhere, except … He waves farewell to the plumbers, dresses in his leathers and walks outside. Sunshine, at last, has turned the puddles of mud to polished amber.

He rides straight to the Greenes'. Mr G's blue Holden ute, its open tray neatly covered with a tarpaulin, perches in its spot on the gravelled drive. He must be at home, then.

Teddy's motor bike is propped against the wall of the house, like he was in a hurry when he arrived and didn't waste time kicking out the stand. Alf chews his bottom lip, parks up behind the ute and tears off his hat and gloves as he marches to the front door.

Maggie, in her nurse's uniform, opens it to his knock: red-eyed, strained pale face, her black curls escaping from where they'd started the day neatly pinned under her cap.

'What's going on?' Alf's voice tightens in fear.

'It's Dad.' Maggie holds the door wide for Alf to step into the passage. 'Heart attack, this morning. Thank God he was at home and not driving, or already at work.'

Alf's own heart lurches.

'I should have come earlier, Mags, I –'

'How were you to know?' She walks ahead of him, the smell of cigarette smoke strengthening as they approach the kitchen. 'Mum called the ambulance and then Teddy at the shop. By the time Teddy got here, Dad was on his way to hospital.'

'Where've they taken him?'

'The Royal.' She swings about at the door. 'I found out when he was admitted. They told me he needed emergency surgery and sent me home to be with Mum. We're waiting for a call, see how the surgery went.'

Mrs Greene, in her dressing gown and without her normal heavy makeup, is upright on a chair with an overflowing ashtray and a half-drunk cup of tea before her. She peers at Alf through slitted, puffy eyes.

'Sorry we couldn't tell you, Alf. It's been … it's been …' She pulls a crumpled hankie from a capacious pocket and blows her nose. 'What we going to do, Maggie, if Dad …?'

'He'll come through, Mum. He's strong.' Maggie kneels beside her mother, patting her arm as Mrs Greene reaches for a cigarette. 'I'll make us another cuppa.'

Alf remembers the bike propped against the wall outside. 'Where's Teddy?'

'Fetching milk and more cigarettes.' Maggie presses her lips together, scoops the kettle off the stove and fills it at the sink.

Above the noise of running water, Alf hears the front door open and bang shut. Teddy strides in, brushing past Alf with a nod. He sets the packet of cigarettes by his mother's elbow and pats her shoulder.

'Thanks for coming, Alf.' Teddy folds his arms across his chest. 'I was going to ride round to yours soon as I could. Saves me a trip.'

'Sorry to hear what's happened.' Alf remains standing. The Greenes have been as much family as his own parents since the days he and Teddy played and fought in the alleyways of East London before the war. Yet this is different, like he's intruding.

'Yeah.' Teddy clamps his hands to the back of a chair. 'Waiting for a call, Maggie probably said.'

'Anything I can do?' Alf needs to be useful, to earn his place here in the intimacy of the kitchen with its pink cupboards and swept, grey floor.

'You can let Raine know what's happening. She'll be expecting me home soon, and don't want to worry her.' He glances at his mother and at Maggie, who's pouring spitting water into a teapot. 'Tell her I'll stay here until we hear from the hospital, however long it takes. Tell her not to worry.'

As well tell an elephant to forget. Alf nods anyway. 'I can do that.' He returns his hat to his head, pulls on his gloves.

'Quick cuppa first?' Maggie lifts a cup.

'Nah. I'll have one with Raine. As Teddy says, don't want to worry her.'

⋄⋄⋄⋄⋄

A winter dusk is settling in, all crisp shadows since the rain dried. Alf drives the bike hard, weaving through the evening traffic, practising the words 'Teddy's fine' to make sure they'll be at the top of his mind when he arrives.

'Alf! Lovely! Wasn't expecting you.' Raine gazes up the road from the front step. 'Teddy's not home yet. Running late.'

Alf, hat and gloves in hand, rumples his hair. 'That's what I've come about –'

Raine steps back, eyes wide. 'Teddy?'

Damn. All his practice.

'Teddy's fine.' He ushers Raine into the house. 'It's Mr G. Had a heart attack –'

'No!'

'He's in the Royal, in surgery. I've come to tell you Teddy'll stay with his mum and Maggie until the hospital calls.'

'Uncle Alf!' Stevie roars down the hall and throws himself at Alf, who lifts him with a grunt.

He pretends to stagger, sets Stevie on the bare boards. 'You grow too quick! Much too heavy for me to lift! Mummy feeding you iron weights?'

Stevie giggles. 'Course not, silly.'

Raine squats, takes hold of Stevie's hands. 'I need you to go into the lounge and keep an eye on Jenny, please. I need to talk to Uncle Alf.'

Alf tells what he knows. Raine leaves him to watch the kids while she goes to the phone box on the corner to ring the Greenes' house. Maggie answered, Raine reports to Alf. They're still waiting. Raine talked to Teddy, passed on her kindest sympathies to Mrs Greene.

She crosses her arms across her chest. 'I pray, pray, pray he pulls through.'

Walking in the Rain

They sit at the kitchen table, Alf eating the sausages, mashed potatoes and peas Raine had prepared for Teddy. The kids ate earlier, have been put to bed and read to by Alf. When Raine came to kiss them good night, she explained that Daddy is staying with Nana Greene tonight because Papa Greene isn't well, and she and Maggie need Daddy's help.

Stevie was curious. 'Aunt Maggie's a nurse. What does she need Daddy for? He's useless when we're sick.'

Raine squeezed his pyjama-clad shoulder. 'They're worried, like we're worried when you or Jenny are ill, and he wants to be there to make them less worried.'

'Hmm.' Stevie tucked teddy under the blankets and received his kiss without further question.

In the kitchen, Raine rests her elbows either side of her unfinished dinner and cups her chin in her hands. 'A lovely man, always kind to me, stuck up for me when … well, you were there, Alf.' Her lips quiver. 'He can't die.'

'He won't die.'

'No, he won't, and I'll have to get over my dislike of hospitals all over again, visit him, take the kids to cheer him up.'

She stares above Alf's head to a spot on the wall, doubtless remembering visits to her father in the same hospital. And the last visit, the day of the Christmas Pageant. Alf never met Raine's father. Neither did Teddy.

'I miss Pop every day.' Raine returns her gaze to the living. 'If Mr G comes through, he won't be able to work for months. How will Mrs Greene cope?'

'She has Maggie, they'll manage. There'll be money from the Housing Trust too, don't worry.' He sighs. 'Means Maggie and Arthur's wedding will have to wait, again.'

'Poor Maggie.' Raine runs with the change of subject. 'She's waited so long already, and all because of this house obsession Arthur has.'

'Mmm.'

Alf plans to add to his 'Mmm', except Raine, elbows still on the table, presses her palms together and peers at him. 'Arthur's right.'

'Right? About his house obsession?' Alf is confused.

'No. About you going someplace else, restart your batteries.' The corners of her mouth curve up. 'Not that I'd compare you to an old car, Alf, only …' She breathes out, catches and holds his gaze, which he's trying to keep neutral despite the urge to protest. 'You're in danger of wasting your life away here. And now … well, with Mr G not able to work, hopefully not forever … it's the perfect time.'

'What makes you think I'm wasting my life?' Her words hurt, because Alf has a deep sense they might be true. 'Not everyone has to marry, have kids, buy an old house at the beach to do up.' He's on the defensive and if it wasn't Raine, he'd raise his voice.

'True.' Raine reaches across to stroke Alf's hand lying on the table, the same motherly way she touched Stevie's shoulder earlier. 'You should have someone, Alf, you deserve happiness too. And that someone might need to be found elsewhere.'

Alf squirms, his skin tingling at Raine's touch and the way his thoughts jump to Nurse June.

'I'm happy enough.' What he means is, he's more or less content. Or he was, until first Arthur, then Raine, started on him.

Raine raises her eyebrows. 'Enough?'

He brushes his hand along the wooden surface of the table. She's a witch, seeing right into his head.

'It doesn't need to be the mountains.' Raine is eager, planning Alf's future and his search for love in fields far distant. 'There's work for electricians all over the country if you don't fancy snow and slush.' She giggles. 'Wouldn't blame you, not after last time.'

Last time, which if things had turned out differently, Alf would be sitting here eating a meal Raine cooked for him, not Teddy. He flushes, uncomfortable, not wanting to dredge up what belongs firmly in the past. Besides, the kitchen, with its ironing board leaning on a crumbling wall and dishes piled in the stained stone sink, is hardly a place for romance. Anyway, Raine's trying to get rid of him, not lure him into temptation.

His shoulders stiffen. 'I'll think about it.' He lowers his head as if chastised, peers up with a teasing boyishness, he hopes. 'If I promise to give it proper thought, you'll stop carrying on like Arthur? No more trying to send me off into the big, bad world?'

Raine doesn't return his playfulness. She stands, pushes her chair in. 'If you did go, we'd miss you, of course.' She glances towards the door. 'I'm going to call again. There must be news by now.'

'No, I'll go. It's late and dark and cold. You stay here.'

He strides down the hall, grabs his jacket and pulls open the front door. A chill wind gusts energetically about him, swirling discarded cigarette packs and lolly wrappers above the footpath. Alf bends his head into the gusts and strides to the phone box. It's good to have a purpose.

Maggie answers on the first ring and Alf expects to be told there's no news and to get off the line.

'It's me. What's happening?'

'Just got off the phone this second, good timing.'

Alf's hopes rise at the lightness in her voice.

'He's pulled through the op, waiting for him to come out of the anaesthetic, but all signs are good.'

'Great news. How's your mum?'

'On her second packet of fags and swimming in tea. Relieved as heck. Teddy's about to go home, and you should too. Thanks, Alfie. You're a terrific friend.'

Alf mutters that's what friends are for and hangs up. The rain has returned, sharp needles harried on all sides by the wind, pricking his face. He squeezes his eyes and walks back to the house, grumbling about 'terrific friends' while the past shoves its embarrassment right in his face.

That conversation with Raine, in the cabin in the hills, when Teddy had been discovered skulking in the Snowy Mountains and in no hurry to come home. The conversation where Alf made a total idiot of himself telling Raine he loved her, wanting to be more than 'terrific friends' – her words – is branded in his consciousness for all time. It slides through his head, as fresh as if it was yesterday. And here he is, 'terrific friend' to Raine, to Maggie, to all of them, to the end of his days.

Is that how June would have come to see him too? The notion rears up in his tired brain, unbidden. Blast Arthur, and Raine too, putting ideas in his head where they're sprouting like spring blossom into impossible dreams. He stomps on a cigarette pack, kicks it into the gutter where it eddies in the rushing water before being swept away.

Impossible dreams or not, Alf confesses that Arthur is right. Raine is right. He needs a kick up the backside to jump start his batteries. He has to get himself in hand and get a life. One not dependent on weekly bouts of domesticity and predictable, repetitive work forever.

He makes his decision.

Chapter Four

THE PERSISTENT SNOW LIES BANKED against kerbs and hedges. The bustle at the hospital was also persistent, and June spent her shift hurrying from one emergency to the next while trying to remain coolly calm for the sake of her patients. Her legs ache, and she's hungry. Earlier, she mentally roamed the contents of her one-shelf larder and has supplied herself with fresh bread to go with the remaining eggs from her last visit to the grocery store.

Hugging the half-loaf to her, she turns into a street lined with old houses and tall trees. Someone has cleared a path, and June's boots remain dry for the remainder of her short journey home. The stone house, built around the turn of the century, is wide and deep and divided into four flats. June's flat faces the street, with a narrow strip of garden to the front and side. Her neighbours are a young couple with a baby; a single woman who does hairdressing from home; and a family of four taking up the largest, two-bedroom place. June rarely sees any of them.

The telephone in the shared hallway rings as she inserts her key into the lock and pushes open the heavy front door. She sets her shopping on the hall table and picks up the black handset.

'Hello, Cooma 463.'

'June! Got you straight off, thank God.' Peter's voice has discarded the frosty tone of the night of her refusal to stay. While they haven't spoken since his clipped 'Suit yourself' response, his tone carries no grudge. 'Weather's finally improved, streets are clearing. Mum's happy to stay with the kids, which means I can wander over your way, take you to the Royal, or the Cooma, for a drink, something to eat.'

Making amends. Also encouraging his mother's all-too-keen approval of her son's new girlfriend. June frequently wonders what the junior Mrs Adams was – is – like, that her mother-in-law so quickly abandoned her. She guesses it's understandable in the circumstances. Doubtless, Mrs Adams senior would be happy to fill June in on the bits Peter hasn't shared, should the woman be given half a chance. June has avoided doing so.

'It's been a long day.' She rubs her calf muscle with a sore foot.

'Needn't be a late one. I can have you home and tucked up early if bed is what you need.' The teasing tone makes her smile. 'Anyway, I can't let Mum be late. She'll be wanting her own bed early too.'

The idea of being fed a decent meal in a warm pub only five minutes' walk from home carries much charm. June concedes.

'I'll meet you at the Royal, 6.30. Bye,' and she hangs up before he can insist he'll collect her, which would likely end up with dinner being an omelette for two, and no warm pub.

He's waiting in the dining room, a beer on the table and a sherry for her. As they've been seeing each other for three months, it's awkward she hasn't yet told him she's not overly fond of sherry. She hangs her coat on the back of her chair, sits and places her handbag on the floor at her feet.

'No problem getting into town?'

He holds the beer out in salutation. 'Cheers. Nope. How was your day?'

June shrugs, sips the sherry. At least this one is a dry sherry, tolerable. 'Busy.'

There's time spent examining the menu, time spent ordering. A wait. Peter fiddles with his cutlery. June takes another sip of her drink.

'Look …' Peter sets the cutlery in place while June looks, eyebrows minutely raised. 'I'm sorry about the other night, I shouldn't have asked. It's just …'

'Just what?' She keeps her voice neutral.

'I like you, a lot. I don't want to ruin this, June.'

Is she meant to fill the pause? It goes on long enough for

Peter to do the honours.

'The kids like you too. They asked the next morning where you were, were kinda disappointed you weren't there.'

June's stomach shrinks. Children missing their mother, wanting a substitute. They don't know her well enough to miss her for herself. She's glad she didn't buy the rainbow petticoat.

'Ah.' She takes another sip of sherry. 'It was more about being snowed in. Did you explain that to them?' She's annoyed at herself. She shouldn't make it seem she wanted to stay, that she cares about the kids. Sweet though they are.

'Yes, yes, I did, and once they looked out the window they understood.' He pushes out his chest. 'They were proud, you being a nurse, a real heroine struggling to your patients through snow and ice.'

Proud?

'You make me sound like a postman.' She laughs.

His steak and chips arrive, together with her ham and pineapple, coleslaw on the side. Another beer for Peter, a water for June.

'Sure you don't want a beer, or a Coke or something?'

June is happy with water. They eat, commenting on how well the steak has been cooked, how tasty the ham is, and June says thank you for not having to eat omelette two nights in a row. They both laugh.

When the plates are cleared, June asks for a cup of tea. Peter nurses his beer. The chat is kept to impersonal things, like how Peter will take on more tradespeople, if he can find them, to keep up with the demands of all this new housing. Shortages of skilled labour all over, despite the number of immigrants heading for the town, and the Scheme.

'Trouble is, most of 'em want to make the big money tunnelling out the mountains.' Peter waves his hand for the bill. 'Staying here and earning less, and safer, money, ain't what they came for.'

June lifts her bag from the floor, digs around inside for

lipstick and mirror. 'You'll find people, I'm sure.'

A quick application, the bill paid, and they walk out to the hotel's lobby.

'Drive you home?'

'Thanks, but no.' June pulls her woollen cap from her coat pocket and stuffs her curls under it. 'You go home to your mum and the kids.' She stops herself saying, 'Tell them hi from me.' Instead she heads to the door, waits for Peter to open it for her, and steps into the cold.

'Look.' She lifts her head to a sky ablaze with stars. 'Beautiful. And very cold, icy too.' She touches Peter's arm. 'Drive carefully.' And turns left along the footpath towards home, where she makes herself cocoa and curls up on the lumpy sofa to drink it, and to think.

Peter is a good man. June is twenty-five and her last boyfriend was nearly a year ago, a breakup she instigated when he proposed all of a sudden, and she found herself saying no. She's heard he's recently married and wishes him and his bride all happiness.

Yes, Peter is a good man. With one major fault. He already has a wife.

◇◇◇◇◇

The air in the hotel bar is grey with cigarette smoke and noisy with the raucous chat of too many men. Alf takes a swallow of his beer and decides it's time he had something to eat. Or should he wait longer for Arthur?

Arthur might not be coming. Alf is lucky, if lucky's the right word, to make it here himself, arriving yesterday on the bus after a long, slow trip. Before he left, he'd written to Arthur, saying he's taking his advice and will join him in whatever camp he's working at, and he planned on arriving in Cooma today, staying at the Royal. He's avoiding the Australian, where he and Raine stayed on the disastrous trip three years ago. This is all about fresh starts and clearing his head – and heart – of old memories. Forging ahead. He takes another, longer, swallow of his beer.

Raine had told him he's mad to go to the mountains.

'I said it's a good idea for you to go someplace else.' Sitting at the table, remains of their meal before them, she threw out her hands. 'I didn't say there. The whole country needs tradespeople!' She huffed, loudly. 'I mean, you could hop over the border to Melbourne, plenty of work to be had.'

Teddy screwed up his mouth in a way supposed to appear worldly-wise. 'Raine's right, mate. I know, I been there, right? It's a hellhole. Don't do it to yourself.'

'Unless …' Raine squinted, pursed her lips. 'This is about Nurse June?'

Alf's attempt to look blank at the name failed. He tapped his fingers on the table either side of his gravy-smeared plate. 'Hardly. Likely she's married with kids by now, after all this time.' Or perhaps not. A thought he kept to himself. 'Honestly' – or not completely dishonestly – 'it's about properly getting away, doing something different.'

Teddy grunted. 'Then you've chosen the right place.'

Raine narrowed her eyes, peered at Alf until he flushed, and let it go.

Having made his decision, Alf is determined to make it a big one. Drama is normally the preserve of Teddy and Raine. This time, it's going to be Alf's drama, adventure anyway. Or it will be if he can get to one of the work camps and not be stuck in Cooma until the spring.

Snippets of conversation from the two blokes beside him infiltrate his hearing.

'…not in or out.'

'That right?'

'Yeah, someone managed to drive a jeep as far as Jindy and telegraphed from there. All the camps are snowed in.'

'Won't be for long. Never is, not with the roads getting better.'

The first speaker snorts. 'Getting better? You mean nowadays roads, of a type, bloody exist at all.'

It explains Arthur. Stuck. As is Alf. Melbourne looks good, if he can face the journey. His stomach rumbles. He needs to eat.

⋄⋄⋄⋄⋄

He declines the barman's offer of another drink and slides off the stool, threads his way between the cigarette smoke and the groups of bantering men to the doorway. He reaches it the same time a couple walk out of the dining room opposite and walk to the main doors. They're a short way ahead of him and neither of them spot him standing there, staring.

It's her, Nurse June. The profile, the blonde curls stuffed under a woollen beanie – definitely her. Alf watches as she waits for the man to open the door, passes through, stares up at the sky and touches the man's arm. She says something and walks out of Alf's view. The man, tall, broad-shouldered, lifts his hat to his head and follows her.

Alf keeps on staring as the door swings shut, and opens to let two giggling young women in. One catches sight of Alf and giggles harder, nudging her friend. He half-smiles and crosses the lobby behind them and into the dining room, although his hunger has sulked off somewhere.

He orders fish and chips, another beer, and thinks about what he saw and why it matters. Arthur's silly teasing truly has gotten to him. Alf's introspection is honest, and he confesses to himself that, yes, perhaps – a small perhaps, he kids himself – part of the reason for coming here was to see those blonde curls, blue eyes, and June's kindly smile.

He'll go to the hospital tomorrow, look her up, say hi. It's the polite thing to do.

If she's still there.

If the scene he just witnessed is anything to go by, June might be married after all, as he said to Raine, which means it's unlikely she's working.

He sets down his cutlery, eats a few chips, leaves the rest. A small, hard stone of disappointment has lodged in his stomach. He's tired, needs sleep. He levers himself up from his seat and heads to the bar to pay for his meal. Tomorrow will bring what tomorrow brings.

◇◇◇◇◇

'Glad the snow's melting.' The waitress places the teapot on the table and screws up her small nose. 'Pretty rare, what we had the last few days.'

Alf's view of blue sky through the dining room's long window is hindered first by the heavy red velvet curtains, and secondly by the wide verandah. The road is wet, dirty piles of slush melting across its surface.

He hmms. 'Does this mean people can get in and out of the camps?'

The girl wipes her hands on her white apron. 'The higher ones'll be bad for a few days yet.' She pulls a notepad and pencil from a side pocket, poises as if about to take his order.

Alf opens his mouth to say he'll have bacon and eggs, toast, just as the girl waves the pencil and frowns. 'You expecting to go up there, looking for work?'

'Yes.'

'You have to sign on at the Authority office, did you know?'

He didn't. Arthur is going to guide him through the ropes, when he turns up. If he turns up.

'Ah, thanks. I'm waiting for a mate to arrive, been here since the beginning, supposed to be holding my hand through all this.'

The girl's pencilled brows rise and she takes a step back, causing Alf to reconsider his use of the hand-holding phrase. Really?

'Can I order breakfast? Before tackling the office?'

'They don't open 'til nine.'

It's eight. He might not get breakfast until nine at this rate.

As it is, he's in his room within thirty minutes. A middle-aged rotund woman with a scarf covering rows of curlers in her hair is making the bed. She glances up, gives Alf a nicotine-stained beam. 'Won't be long, love. Then you can have it back.'

Stepping around the basket of piled linen on the floor, Alf returns the smile. 'No problem. Need to fetch my coat and I'll be out your way. Thanks.'

He grabs his leather cycle jacket from its hook on the door, wondering if a warmer jacket, fleece-lined, might be a good idea if he's planning on staying. Shrugging his arms into the sleeves, he nods to the woman who doesn't notice because she's bed-making, and wanders along the fusty-smelling passage and down the stairs to the lobby.

Alf hands the room's big heavy key on its wooden holder to the receptionist, who answers his question about the location of the Authority's office by pointing north.

'It's a bit of a walk. Best to catch the bus, though it doesn't open 'til nine.'

Alf says he knows, and adds that he's not keen on a bus after spending two days on one, and it'll be good to walk. He'll have a browse in the shop windows on the way.

She giggles and tells him her mum spends a lot of her day peering through shop windows, rarely going in.

'Doesn't like to spend money, still thinks it's the war and rationing, I reckon.' She grins and morphs into a rapid subject change. 'By the way, how long are you planning to stay?' She examines the wide, ruled book spread out on the desk before her. 'Not a problem right now, plenty of rooms.'

'Ah, good. Truth is, not sure. Don't expect it'll be for long.' Alf holds his hands out. 'Depends how quick I can get out to the Scheme.'

'Not long then. They're hungry for workers, all sorts.'

As Alf turns to leave, the receptionist calls after him. 'I'd buy myself a warmer jacket if I was you. Need it up there.'

He lifts a hand in acknowledgement and pushes the door

open, walking into the crisp, cold morning to join people hurrying to work and loud groups of dawdling kids in school uniforms. A few cars – most of them elderly, all of them streaked with mud – inhabit the wide street. Others are parked at an angle to the footpath which is covered here and there with shop verandahs sporting colourful hoardings. A rural town waking up to busyness and purpose.

Alf takes his time over the longish walk. He spots cafés likely to be cheaper than eating at the hotel, sees the cinema is playing *Roman Holiday*, and finds a menswear shop with every inch of window space taken up with trousers, shoes, ties, shirts, and jackets. His leather is warm enough as long as the sun's out, but he'll stop by on the way back, invest in something cosier.

Or should he? Hardly needs a heavy jacket at home. Or Melbourne, if he decides to go there. He'll hold off, see what happens.

At a sprawling intersection, he passes a signpost pointing to the hospital and stops on the corner to gaze along the street where big trees weep snow. Too far to see the old stone building with its picket fence, his brain supplies the image. Together with the memory of surviving on tea and biscuits while Raine and Teddy between them made a tangled botch of explaining what was going on – that is, nothing – between Teddy's wife and Teddy's best mate, that is, Alf. He can laugh about it now. Pretty much.

There's another, more pleasant, memory: Nurse June's practical sympathy and friendship.

He stares around, vaguely wondering if he might bump into her, like last night. Cooma's not a big place, must happen all the time. He gazes along the street. There's no rush to be at the Authority's office. He could call in at the hospital, ask if June Lovell works there, or is even June Lovell these days. He ignores the disappointment which a night's sleep failed to dislodge. He lifts his shoulders, defiant. So what if she isn't? It would be polite and pleasant to catch up with her, tell her how things are going in more detail than Arthur did. Assuming she'd be interested.

Alf draws in a breath, lets it out. Her hand on the man's arm last night … an intimate touch. He'll call at the hospital later. It's early in the day for calling on people out of the blue.

The shops dwindle once he's past the intersection. A cold wind off the mountains harries pedestrians and Alf quickens his steps, needing warmth and something to concentrate on apart from mooning over yesteryear.

The office is in a side street, and by the time Alf arrives, a short queue of would-be workers has formed at the wooden counter. A clerk is talking to a job applicant. Behind the clerk, the space is filled with small desks where men and women deal with folders of maps, concentrate on writing, type furiously or, in one case, talk on the telephone. The noise is muted, excepting the typewriter clacking away with no regard for anyone's thinking ability. In the far corner, a tall man in a suit peers through the open doorway of a partitioned office.

Alf's turn in the queue arrives. He puts on a serious, job-seeking face.

'I'm an electrician, looking for work on the Scheme. Wondering what's available.'

The clerk nods. 'Always need electricians. Trouble is, we can't get anyone up there for a few days yet.' He places his hands on the counter. 'I'll give you a form, fill it in and bring it here tomorrow. We can take it from there.'

He bends, takes a form from under the counter, hands it over and peers behind Alf to summon the next applicant. Alf steps aside and wanders through the door to make the return journey. He folds the form in two, slips it into his jacket pocket.

He can't help thinking if this is an omen – like the disruptive snow, like June's hand on the man's arm – telling him he shouldn't be here at all.

Chapter Five

THE KIDS ARE IN BED, having had a story from June. She sits on the square-cushioned Danish sofa in the living room and reaches out to take the cup of tea Peter made for her.

He plumps down beside her, salutes her with his beer. 'Thanks for the story, they love bedtime reading.'

'No problem, they're good listeners.' June likes these kids. They're bright, full of questions, eager to talk. It wouldn't be too hard to love them.

She drinks her tea, turns to face Peter, her back pressed to the sofa's slim wooden arm. 'Can I ask you something?' It's been on her mind too long.

'Sure, go ahead.' He shrugs. 'Sounds serious.'

'It is serious.' She pauses, notes the frown which comes and goes across his forehead. 'You've never said what happened to their mother, to Leah, apart from the fact she's not here.' She sets the cup and saucer on the teak coffee table. 'Do you mind telling me more?'

Peter takes a long swallow of beer, puts the bottle next to June's tea and runs his hand through his hair. June catches the reflection of the action in the wide mirror over the open fire where thick logs crackle warmth.

'Not a lot to tell.' He faces her, his eyes hard. 'I thought everything was wonderful. I thought we were happy, she was happy.' He grimaces. 'Of course, like all women, she had her moody days when I knew to leave her alone.' A pause, and the rest comes rushing out like an apology. 'We didn't fight, never raised our voices to each other. Leah enjoyed furnishing this place when we bought it.' He pats the sofa. 'All the modern stuff to go with the new build.' He slows, rubs his chin. 'Then …' He looks through the door to the passage leading to the children's bedroom. 'Then one day, bit over a year ago, she didn't come home from a trip to Sydney. Supposed to be visiting an old school friend. When I phoned, the friend said she never showed, assumed she'd changed her mind and would write or call.'

June frowns. 'Must have been a worry.'

'Yeah, of course. To disappear ...' He sucks in a breath. 'I went to the police, straight off, because maybe there'd been an accident and no one had been able to contact me. They were good, started looking into it.'

'And?' June understands there was no accident, for if there had been, she wouldn't be sitting on this couch.

Peter throws out his hands, clips the beer bottle and grabs it before it topples. 'A day later a postcard arrives, stamped Sydney GPO, saying she was sorry, and not to worry, she was okay.' His voice is tight. 'The police stopped looking, not interested, more urgent things to do.' He swallows, drops his eyes to his lap before bringing his head up. 'And that's all there is to tell. She's gone.'

It's a defiant stance, and June senses the hurt behind it. She has more questions, selfish ones like, where does this leave me? You're a married man, what future is there for us? This isn't the time to ask.

'I'm truly sorry. For you, for the kids. Thanks for telling me.' Poor Ben and Debbie. It's amazing they're such good kids.

It helps to learn more, little as it is. It helps to glimpse what this abandoned husband, father, might be feeling. It doesn't make things easier.

She stands, rubs her face with her hands. 'I need to go, early shift in the morning.'

Peter pushes himself from the sofa, wraps his arms around her, and June fears he's going to ask her to stay. He draws her close, and she lays her head on his chest, liking his solidity, the prickle of his woollen jumper against her cheek.

'Thanks for listening. I've always felt there's never been the right time to tell you.' His laugh ruffles her hair. 'It's one of the things I love about you, June. You're straightforward.'

He holds her away from him. 'Now you see why Debbie

and Ben, and me, appreciate having you around. We can rely on you and your common sense.'

'Hmm, thanks. I guess.'

◇◇◇◇◇

The day is clear, cold, and the Authority office is barely open when Alf pushes at the door, happy to see there's no queue. A different clerk takes his form, scans it and sets it on the counter. 'Certificates?'

Alf hands over his documents.

'At least they're in English.' The clerk, an overweight Australian, raises his eyes to the ceiling. 'Means it shouldn't take as long.'

'What shouldn't take as long?'

'Processing and allocating, deciding where you're to go, unless you've an overriding wish for a particular camp?'

'Ah.' Alf has assumed he'll go with Arthur. He's a grown man, however, a big boy. 'Not really. I guess they know where they need us. I'll let them decide.'

'Great. We're likely to have you sorted in about a week.'

'A week?'

'Yeah, it'd normally be quicker, except this bloody snow has slowed everything down.' He looks past Alf as the door opens to a new arrival. 'Come back then.'

Alf steps aside, turns and wanders out into the cold air.

What should he do? A week is too long to stay at the Royal. He doesn't have those kind of funds, and he's supposed to be here saving money not spending it. Saving it for what exactly? He lets the question slide. He could go to June's aunt's boarding place, where he stayed last time. Or find another boarding house. There must be plenty about.

And a short-term job. He walks into town, looking out for boarding houses along the way.

By the evening, he's bought himself a warmer jacket, heavier trousers, and sorted a place to stay. His landlady, Mrs Beale, is not like June's warmly welcoming aunt, and the old, sprawling house is not as cosily pleasant. Alf doesn't care. Not for a week.

He checks out of the Royal, leaves his suitcase to collect later, and goes to the bar for a beer before heading out to eat at a café he spotted earlier. A little before the end of the working day, the place is empty except for an old man in a corner studying the racing form, cigarette smoke swirling above his bald head, pint in hand. The barman polishes glasses, lining them up ready for the five o'clock rush.

'Wonder if you could help me out with something.' Alf pushes his empty glass towards the barman for a refill.

'Sure, if I can.'

'Looking for short-term work, daily stuff, electrical, worked on building sites before I came up here. Any suggestions?'

'Not going to the Scheme?'

'Eventually, but they say it'll take a week and I can't afford to play tourist for a week.'

'Fair enough.' The barman slides Alf's refilled glass across the bar. 'Shouldn't be a problem, plenty of work around.' He looks up as a group of men walk through the door, taking off their hats as they come. 'Look there, just the ticket.' He tilts his head at the group. 'Peter Adams' boys. He's pretty much the biggest builder about. I'll introduce you and they can tell you all about the boss.' He smirks. 'The business side anyway.'

⋄⋄⋄⋄⋄

June's early morning shift goes on into the late morning and continues into the late afternoon, her hours extended by a drawn-out birth for a first-time mother who decided June's hand was the most solid object to latch onto. The baby safely delivered, and the pacing father informed he has a healthy son, June is free to leave.

In the nurses' staff room, she fills the kettle and puts it on to boil. A hot drink before heading into the winter dusk and her chilly flat will ease her into the evening. While she waits, her thoughts go to Peter's too-short tale of his missing wife. Most of those thoughts involve the hardness in his eyes and his unwillingness to talk further. He's hurting, of course. What isn't he saying? What more is there? Because a young mother doesn't up and leave her children for no reason.

'That kettle for the two of us?' Libby breezes into the room, pulling her cap off as she goes, releasing her golden red hair and sending pins falling to the floor. 'Damn.' She bends to collect the pins, straightens and grins at June. 'Yes? Tea for two?'

'Of course. Just having a last one before heading home.'

'Lucky you. I've hours to go yet.' Libby shares this news with a pout. 'Seeing Peter tonight?'

'No. He and the kids are at his mum's this evening. I was invited, but …' June measures tea leaves into a teapot, lets the sentence wander off.

'But?' Libby pulls out a chair and sits with a sigh. 'Good to get off my feet.' She wags a finger. 'Why not go to visit the mum?'

June pours boiling water into the pot and searches for the right words, glad to have someone to test her feelings on. Not that Libby is any Agony Aunt, although she'd love the accolade.

'He's still married, Peter. His wife is out there somewhere.'

'Hmm. Wondered when that would come up.' Libby rubs her calf muscles, screws up her lightly freckled nose.

'You know what happened?'

'Some.'

'Ah.' June sets the pot on the table and searches out clean mugs. She places them by the pot, finds milk in the fridge, and sits opposite Libby. 'Well? What can you tell me?'

Libby pours, frowning. 'Peter and Rob – you've met him, right? My big brother, married with kids. Anyway, they were in the same year at school and afterwards played football together, in the days Peter and Leah were first married. He met her in Sydney, somehow, somewhere.'

'She's from Sydney?'

'Yeah. A stranger when she came here, and Rob asked me to help Peter out, be a friend to her.' Libby blows on her hot tea, stares through the darkening window.

'What's she like?'

Libby sniffs. 'Not easy to be friends with. Treated us all like country bumpkins, going on about all the *culture* in the Big Smoke of the city, unlike here.' She clasps the mug with two hands. 'We never became friends, saw each other occasionally. She mellowed after Ben was born. Had her own clique by then, other mums from the new houses.'

'Why did she leave?'

'How would I know? I bet it was nothing Peter did. He's nice, the sweetest, and he didn't deserve what she did to him.' Her eyes stray again to the window.

June agrees Peter is sweet. 'He's kind, for sure. And a great dad. His kids adore him, poor little buggers.' Their loss affects her far more than Peter's.

'He was besotted with her, gave her anything she wanted, and look how she treated him.' Libby gazes at June, green eyes merry. 'You're a lucky woman, June Lovell. Peter's quite a catch.'

'Shame he's married, huh?'

The words repeat themselves in a loop as June walks home, her coat wrapped tightly about her against a cold wind, her nurse's cap replaced with a woollen beanie.

Why is she wasting her time? She should move on.

Peter's quite a catch.

Libby's right. June likes Peter, a lot. She likes his grounded presence, the way he loves his children, the way he treats her, thoughtful, kind. And Ben and Debbie are in desperate need of a new mother. One who'll stick around.

Chapter Six

A SECRETARY, DARK HAIR IN a ponytail, types at speed in a functional room which could, with grace, be labelled 'reception'. Two hardback chairs keep each other company along a wall under a window, and face an area holding metal filing cabinets, a table piled with plans, and the small desk containing the secretary. An electric heater warms the young woman's feet. The rest of the room is chilly.

She pauses, hands curled above the keyboard, ready to take up where they stopped.

'Can I help you?'

'Looking for Mr Adams.' Alf takes off his hat. 'Met these blokes who said he might have work for an electrician, temporary work.'

'He's not here. Expecting him soon if you want to wait?'

Alf has nowhere else to be, and he needs the work. 'Sure.'

'Take a seat.' Her fingers clamp onto the keys and the clatter resumes.

It's not long before Peter Adams strides in, glances at Alf while the secretary explains, and invites him into the partitioned office in a corner.

Alf sees the photo as he takes the offered seat on the other side of a cluttered desk: a photo of June in a silver frame, between a folder and a pile of plans. There's another photo on the desk, of two cute kids, a boy and a girl. His brain takes in both images, holding them until he can work out what it means.

He flicks his eyes from the photos to Peter. He must be the man he saw with June his first night in Cooma. Her husband. The shape and size are right, given Alf had a rear view.

His brain lurches into action. She couldn't have been married when he was here with Raine and Teddy, could she? Not given what happened … He shies away, takes his thoughts in a different direction. The kids can't be hers, not possible, and her name was Lovell, not Adams.

While his thoughts spin like a juggler's balls, he manages to get his request out.

'A few days' work until orders from HQ come through, hey?' Peter chuckles. 'Not unusual, and often as not the blokes stay on.' He shrugs. 'Reckon it's more comfortable and a lot safer working in town than up in those tunnels. Especially in this.' He gestures at the big window seen through the glass partition.

A light smattering of snow dusts the rooftops and trees. It won't settle, the feathery flakes chivvied away by a cold wind as Alf sits opposite the photo of June.

'Yeah, I can see how they might change their minds.' Alf might change his own. 'But it's good money and nowhere to spend it. I've a friend been working up there since the beginning, and he's pretty much saved up for a house. A wedding gift for his impatient soon-to-be bride.'

'A great way to get funds together, for sure. And as it happens, I've a heap of small jobs waiting for a good sparky, so welcome aboard, Alf.' Peter Adams leans forward and stretches out his hand for Alf to shake.

Alf rises, shakes the hand above the photo.

'June, right?' He blurts it. 'A nurse, at the hospital.'

Peter's eyebrows go up. He falls into his chair. 'Yeah, it's June. How do you know her?'

Alf explains, briefly, how June was on duty the night of the accident, how helpful she'd been, they all remembered her fondly, he and Teddy and Raine. He leaves it there, which is where it should be left, because that's all there was. Almost.

'Sounds like June.' Peter beams. 'My fiancée.' He gestures at the children. 'My kids, Ben and Debbie. They adore her, can't wait for her to be their mum.'

Fiancée? As good as married. Alf's too polite to ask about their real mum. He assumes a tragedy, death, poor mites. June will be a great mum to them. Anyone with her sympathetic eyes, the way she can lay a hand on your sleeve and make you believe all the world is good – yes, June will be a wonderful mother.

Peter is writing on a form and takes no notice of Alf's silence. He signs the form, hands it to Alf, who takes it without reading it.

'Fill that in and give it to the foreman, Tony Stubbs, at the site tomorrow. The address is there.' He points at the form. 'Eight o'clock, don't be late. I'll sort it with payroll.'

'Thanks.' Alf forces a casual tone. 'Appreciate it. And, um, say hello to June from me, if she remembers us at all.' His neck warms at the lie, given what Arthur told him. He's not going into all that, not with her fiancé.

The walk to the boarding house is punctuated with a stop to buy a lunch box and the makings of sandwiches for tomorrow. He buys a thermos too, confident his landlady will fill it for him at breakfast. Coats, trousers, lunch boxes, thermoses – he's accumulating belongings fast, settling in. In less than a week. He's doing it automatically, going with the flow, not thinking too hard. No change there then.

When he's in the boarders' lounge – which he has to himself and can listen to the wireless, dialling back and forth for music he likes – he finds himself spluttering with laughter like a crazy person. Despite Arthur's teasing words, Alf hadn't truly believed a beautiful woman like June would be waiting in Cooma, daily wishing for his return. A secret, tiny place deep inside him had, however, waved a tiny flag of optimism, nurturing impossible dreams. Now, assuming he could summon the courage to talk to her, to search for any flame of interest, he'd be an utter bastard and a home breaker if anything, miraculously, happened between them.

Raine and Teddy all over again? Except this time, he won't make a fool of himself. He'll fold his flag of optimism and respectfully lay it to rest alongside those dreams, deep inside his heart, which has been bruised enough.

'Met an old friend of yours today.' Peter spears a boiled potato and waves it in the air.

June looks up from slicing her roast beef. Peter is treating her to an early dinner out, followed by a film. *Roman Holiday* has finally reached the mountains, and June adores Audrey Hepburn. It's good to be looked after, treated with dinners and films on a regular basis. Another tick in the box for Peter Adams.

'Oh, who?'

'Alf Hall. New in town, came looking for temporary work before going to the Scheme.'

June's stomach performs a tiny flip. Alf is here? How coincidental, given she thought about him a couple of days ago, when the ambulance arrived in the snow. And there was his friend she bumped into a couple of weeks ago, when she asked after Raine and Teddy, and Alf.

'Hardly an old friend.' She smiles. 'If it's who I think it is.' Of course it is. Why does she need to cover up, as if Alf is a guilty secret?

'Said you helped some mates of his out a few years ago, at the hospital.'

'Yes, yes, sounds like the right person.' She sets down her knife and fork because her hands have started a tiny tremulous shaking while her stomach insists on fluttering. What on earth? 'Quite a palaver.' Her smile grows wider. 'Something of a romantic tangle going on.'

The pretence at humour drains away. Alf's pain, his foot slowly making circles on the ward's polished floor. Nothing funny there.

'It all got sorted, I believe.' She slices another bite of beef. 'Why is he here? Don't recall him falling in love with our fair town.'

And if he's here, why hasn't he come to the hospital to say hello? Given what they went through. He wrote afterwards, to thank her for her help. No mention of anything beyond that. She replied, full of news, wanting to stay in touch, but the gap between his letters lengthened and their content grew sparser until they shrank to nothing. June decided she'd misunderstood Alf's reaction, that day at the lookout above the town, when she reached out to comfort him.

Peter forks up peas, holds the fork above his plate. 'Like most of them, wants to earn a pile of decent money in a short time. Good place to do it. He talked about a friend who's getting married and has saved enough to pretty much buy a house outright.'

'I see.' June believes she does see. Alf, like his friend, has wedding plans and he wants to start married life in comfort. He must be over his infatuation with Raine, found himself a worthy woman.

'I'm happy for him.' She glances at her watch. 'We need to be going. I don't want to be late for Audrey.' Yes, she's happy for Alf. Truly she is.

Chapter Seven

THE WORK IS THE SAME, the noises too: hammering and sawing, shouts of labourers calling up to the bricklayers, wheelbarrows squeaking along temporary boards laid over puddled remnants of snow. It's cold in the windowless, doorless houses which the carpenters, Phil and Tom, are working hard to enclose. Alf enjoys his workmates' bantering company. Big guys with scarred hands, born and bred in Cooma, they tease him about going to the Scheme, how no one up there speaks a word of English and he should stay here where he can at least talk to people. They're flippant, and when Alf asks, seriously, why they haven't taken the chance to earn good money, they tell him they know those mountains too well and why run the risk of joining the list of the dead, short as it is. So far.

During a break, the three of them sit on the floor, Phil and Tom smoking rollups, Alf with his thermos. He pours tea into the metal lid. 'Mate of mine was nearly killed up there, 'bout three years ago.'

'That right?'

'Land Rover bringing him and another guy in to Jindy got pushed off the track by a sliding frontloader. Snowy and slippery.'

Phil blows out a ragged smoke ring. 'Everyone survive?'

'Yeah, luckily. Touch and go for a while.'

There's a moment's silence during which Alf thinks about everything else that was touch and go at the time. He gulps the lukewarm tea, screws the lid into place and hauls himself to his feet. 'Back to work. Reckon I'll finish the first fix here today, find out from Stubbs where next.'

He heads to the living room, steps through the doorless opening. 'Last room to do, let's see what –'

Phil gives a shout. 'Watch out!'

Alf half turns, still walking forward. His foot finds only air. He crashes to the floor, landing with a whumpf on his stomach, knocking the air from his lungs. His left leg is in a boardless gap, his right leg splayed behind him across the threshold. Searing pain courses through his left ankle.

Tom's there first, stepping over Alf's prone body to squat next to him, asking if he's all right.

'No.' Alf tries to push himself up and fails, yelping at the pain. 'Think it's broken.' Bloody hell. It's the last thing he needs, not being able to work. This whole idea is going belly up.

'Here.' Phil bends to Alf's side, jerks his head at Tom. 'You take the other side, careful, and we'll haul him out of there and take a look.'

Phil explains he was a hospital orderly in the war, where he saw plenty of injuries far worse than broken ankles. He carefully pulls off Alf's shoe and lifts his trouser leg. Alf stares at the purple swelling.

'Hospital for you, mate. I'll take you there.' He turns to Tom. 'Tell Stubbs, will you?'

◇◇◇◇◇

Phil's battered ute, its open back loaded with timber and tools, swings through the hospital's iron gates and parks at the front of the old, red brick building. The sight takes Alf back three years. Same gloomy weather, same hospital. He snorts softly, gives a reluctant, experimental twist of his ankle, and winces.

Phil supports him as he stumbles up the two steps and across the verandah into the foyer. A grey-haired receptionist is on the phone. She glances across at them, speaks hurriedly into the receiver and replaces the handpiece with a click.

'Problem?' She's already dialling. 'Hang on, someone will be right here.'

Lowering Alf into a chair, Phil addresses the woman. 'Might be a broken ankle. Bad swelling anyway.'

Bad pain too. Alf's about to ask if it's possible to have aspirin, when June Lovell hurries in.

For a reason he doesn't understand, Alf flushes, guilt

tickling his gut like he's been caught with his hand in the biscuit tin. She stops, frowns briefly, turns the frown into a professional smile. Her blue eyes are cool.

'Well, look who's the patient this time. Nice to see you, Alf, and what have you done to yourself?'

No deep surprise at his presence. Peter Adams must have told her he was here.

'Ankle.' He stretches his shoeless leg out, adds his own greeting. 'I hope you're well, Nurse Lovell?'

She raises her eyebrows at the formality, and Alf wishes he could re-say the clumsy greeting. She'll think him unfriendly, cold, adding insult to injury in not coming to see her.

'Fine, thank you.' June is politely distant. She gently prods the swelling, asks him to wriggle his toes, arch his foot. She gives him the professional smile and Alf's pain spreads beyond his swollen ankle. His face is hot, his skin sticky with sweat. Great way to come back into June's life.

'We'll do an x-ray, but my suspicion is it's a sprain, not broken.' She crosses her arms, nods. 'Wrapped up tight, you'll be able to get around, if slowly, and on firm surfaces.'

It's better news than a break, but firm surfaces? Alf has his own suspicions, and they're about the lack of firm surfaces in the Scheme's camps. He wriggles in the chair, which seems too hard, too small. 'Ah, good, I guess. How long before it heals?'

'Depends how bad it is.' She turns away. 'Let's organise the x-ray.'

Phil leaves, with a promise to return shortly to take Alf to the boarding house. Alf's company is the receptionist – who returns to her paperwork – and his throbbing ankle. His foot rests on a second chair and he sits, eyes closed, his mind carping on his stupid, unenthusiastic greeting. Why wasn't he cheerily friendly, normal? He recalls the light touch of June's hand on his arm the day of Jenny's birth, and conjures the sympathy in her eyes, her openness and practical help. And the day she led him to the lookout above the town, what passed between them. He's upset her, acting like an ungrateful stranger.

June returns with a wheelchair and pushes Alf to the x-ray room.

'I saw your friend … Arthur, right? A few weeks ago. He told me Raine and Teddy and the kids are doing well.'

Her tone is light, chatty, one casual acquaintance to the other. Alf's guilt deepens.

'Yes, yes, they are.' He's glad for the chance to make amends. 'Though there's always a drama going on with them.'

'I can imagine.' She laughs softly and Alf is also glad to hear her laugh.

He wants to ask about her engagement, congratulate her, say Peter Adams seems a good man. Something stops him. She doesn't ask him why he's here, in Cooma. He's created a barrier and June is politely tapping at it, not launching a major assault.

They turn into a room heavy with medical equipment fussed over by a young man in a white coat and spectacles.

'Here we are. This is Jimmy, our radiographer.' Jimmy says hello and continues fussing. June walks to the door. 'Someone'll come and collect you when this is done, and we'll bind that ankle, give you painkillers.'

She's gone. Will Alf see her before he leaves the hospital? Before he leaves Cooma? A hole has opened inside him, an empty, unsatisfactory hole.

X-ray done, the ankle is declared sprained, not broken. An orderly wheels Alf to a small room where a red-headed nurse binds the injury and hands him a packet of tablets with instructions to take four a day maximum. She pushes him to the foyer and brings him a cup of tea and two plain biscuits to see him through the wait for his lift to the boarding house. More old memories surface, of surviving for what seemed days on endless cups of tea and biscuits set out in the hospital's waiting room. Until June, noticing, persuaded him to go with her to a café to eat a proper meal.

The red-headed nurse asks about the accident. 'How and where did it happen?'

Alf tells her.

'You're working for Peter Adams? Polo Flat way?'

'Yeah, the new houses.'

She gives a cheeky grin to match the teasing sparkle in her green eyes. Alf grins too, with no idea what's funny.

The nurse twists about as June appears with a file. 'Hey, June.'

June hands the file to the receptionist and briefly talks to her before turning around.

'Yes. Is there something wrong, Libby?' She raises her eyebrows.

'No, all good, a sprain, bandaged. Just that poor Alf here works for your Peter.' Libby sucks in her teeth. 'You should tell him to take better care of his employees.' She looks sideways at Alf, winks. 'Especially the cute ones.'

Alf's neck warms at the unexpected flirting. June blushes too, although she must understand the nurse is joking about her fiancé.

Libby smirks, pats Alf's shoulder and glances towards the front door, which is being pushed open by Phil. 'Looks like your lift is here.'

'Bye, Alf.' June is already leaving. 'Libby, can you give Alf his instructions on what to do to make sure the sprain heals as quickly as possible?'

'Sure.' Libby's eyes crinkle. 'My pleasure.'

◇◇◇◇◇

'He's the guy who was here two, three years ago, right?' Libby questions June over the nurses' room sink where she's washing cups and saucers.

June is drying. She doesn't want this conversation, to think about Alf. Even though she knew he was in town, it was a shock to see him in the hospital. Her emotions seesaw between instinctive pleasure and a need to stifle that pleasure, given he obviously doesn't think enough of her to come by the hospital to say a short hello. She's not going to waste more emotion on him.

'Uh-huh.' A non-committal response.

Libby persists. 'When the fellow had the accident up in the mountains, and his wife had the baby early, and the way Alf paced you would've thought it was his kid. That him?'

'Yes.'

The other nurses had been keen to delve to the bottom of this exciting triangle, and as June had first contact, she was the one silently designated to find out more. It was no burden, given she liked Alf immediately. It was the way he looked out for Raine, his excitement when the baby was born. Like he was the husband, the proud daddy.

And here it comes, the image of Alf at the door of the ward, foot sliding across the polished floor, eyes on the happy family. Her heart aches for him all over again. A wasted aching.

Libby rinses another cup, places it on the draining board. 'He used to be tubbier.'

That's what's different. Alf is leaner, with more muscle and less stomach. Whatever he's been doing these past years, it's been kind to him. June has an urge to rush to the mirror by the coat hooks and check out what the years have done to her. She tells herself not to be stupid. She's hardly a wizened crone.

Libby gives her an appraising look, lips twitching. 'You know, I thought at the time there might be something there between you and him.'

June polishes a cup with extra vigour. 'All in your romantic imagination, my dear.' And in June's, never to be confessed, not now. 'Alf only had eyes for Raine. Raine only had eyes for her missing-now-found-almost-died husband.'

'Poor Alf.' Libby sets the last saucer in the draining rack and pulls the plug. 'Do you think he's here nursing his broken heart?'

Her eyes gleam, and June senses trouble. 'After all this time?' She wipes the saucer. 'Taking unrequited love too far, don't you think?'

'You're right. Alf is definitely ready for love.' Libby wipes her hands on a towel. 'A romantic hero needs a leading lady.' She lifts her chin, presses the towel to her chest. 'And here I am.'

June's stab of irritation makes her snappy. 'He probably has a wife, or girlfriend, stashed at home. Peter says he's come here to save for a house, which suggests you'd be wasting your time.'

'Maybe, maybe not.' Libby lifts her coat and hat from their hook and faces June with a more sombre expression. 'I'm not playing about for the fun of it. He's sweet, cute.' She shrugs. 'If you didn't have your Peter, I'd say you and he would make a great pair. But you do, lucky girl, and I'd like to know Alf better.'

Her Peter? Is he 'her' Peter? June bites her bottom lip.

Libby pushes her arms into her coat sleeves, pulls on her hat. 'I've an idea. Tell Peter he owes Alf a slap-up meal for having a dangerous work site.' Mischief lights her eyes. 'Invite me along, make it a foursome. Come on, help out a friend?'

Despite telling herself she shouldn't be interested, June is curious too, about why Alf is here, whether he's over Raine, is he married, engaged, has a girlfriend. 'Okay, I'll suggest it. Don't build your hopes up. Don't want you falling for a married man.'

Libby titters. 'What, make two of us?'

June can't return the humour. What a hypocrite she is.

Chapter Eight

PETER NEEDS NO PERSUASION TO host a dinner out, teasing June about Libby's less than subtle attempts to cosy up to Alf.

He tilts his chair back, his eyes following the children scurrying from the remains of their meal, shouting about racing each other to Ben's room where a new train set is slowly being assembled. 'He's a good worker, Alf. Turned up this morning leaning on a stick and put in a solid day. Shame he's planning on disappearing soon.'

June says she agrees it's a shame. Although, to herself, she's ambivalent. Tending to Alf at the hospital has stirred emotions she considered well buried, emotions which explain her snappiness to the innocent Libby. Does she wish Alf gone? In all honesty … She collects plates and cutlery, pushing unhelpful, and possibly dangerous, thoughts aside.

'Maybe Libby'll persuade him to stay.' Yes, concentrate on Libby's feelings. Much better idea.

'If anyone can, she's the woman.' Peter gives an amiable snigger.

Dinner is booked for the Cooma Hotel's dining room, and it takes June an age to decide what to wear. She wants to look her best, for Peter's sake.

It's nothing to do with the fact Alf has rarely seen her out of her nurse's uniform. A few times, when she wore trousers and jumpers to show him around Cooma during the week he waited for Teddy and Raine to leave hospital. Over fish and chips or strolling through the older parts of town, Alf had told her bits and pieces of the Teddy and Raine tale – leaving out the parts revealing where his own heart stood. They chatted about how lucky Teddy had been to survive the accident, and June made Alf laugh when she joked about Teddy also being lucky to survive Raine's fury at discovering her husband assumed Alf was the new baby's father. She recalls his laugh had been strained, and he had turned the conversation to other topics, like his and Teddy's life during the Blitz in London.

June shakes her head and drapes a soft burgundy wool dress with a pencil-skirted frock, elbow-length sleeves and a deep V-neck against herself. She twists her body and peers into the mirror in the corner of her bedroom. She doesn't take in the sight. She's seeing the shadow in Alf's eyes back then, the window to what he doubtless believed was the secret cave where his love for Raine lay buried. A shallow grave, June believed at the time. With good reason.

She sighs, decides the dress will do and wonders how shallow the grave is these days. Likely she'll find out soon. Not that it matters.

Peter compliments her extravagantly when he collects her from her flat, telling her how beautiful she is and she should wear this frock more often, it sets off her unflawed skin and golden hair. He's in a particularly upbeat mood, beaming as if Christmas is tomorrow and he's expecting a sack load of gifts.

June is pleased she made the effort, appreciating the flattery, using it to encourage a happy mood for the evening. Three years has possibly been good to her, as it has to Alf. She lets the mood build as they make their way through the linen-draped tables of the dining room to where Libby waits, a glass of white wine in hand. She's made an effort too, in an emerald-green strappy outfit which accentuates her eyes and shiny, wavy hair. June's pleasure at Peter's compliments drowns in a wave of self-doubt dancing a wild jig in her head. Beside a Libby dressed to kill, June might as well be a wizened crone.

'Sorry we're late.' Peter looks around. 'Alf not here yet?' He winks at Libby, the upbeat mood clinging to him like a shiny coat. 'Or have you frightened him off?'

Libby lifts her glass. 'Cheers to you too, Mr Adams.'

'Here he is.' June signals to Alf, who limps across the room propelled by a walking stick, moving fast for a man with a sprained ankle.

He makes his own apologies, which are dismissed, and the four of them settle to study the menu.

June can recite what's on offer in her sleep, and will let Peter choose for her in any case. She holds the off-white piece of cardboard close to her face and sneaks a look over the top to study Alf. What is his story since they last met? She shouldn't be this curious, although surely any questions can be seen as merely polite conversation.

Libby gets there first, not waiting for orders to be taken. 'Tell us everything, Alf, about why you're here. Is there a girl at home, waiting for her new house?'

'New house?' Alf lowers his menu and frowns at Libby.

'You're not here to save money for a house?' Her eyes brighten.

'Well, no.' Alf shakes his head. 'More for a change than anything, see a different part of the world. Or the country, at least.'

'Take part in the great Snowy adventure, be part of history.' Peter's tone is grave, and June is irritated by his pomposity.

'Yeah.' Alf returns to his menu.

Libby keeps the pressure on. 'Wandering fancy free then?'

'I guess.'

June's pulse shouldn't give the tiny jump it does.

A crease flickers between Alf's eyebrows. 'Gave up my flat to come here, stored my stuff and my motorbike at a friend's place.' He glances at June. 'Teddy's.'

June takes the conversational ball. 'Did they stay in the cabin? Raine talked about being up in the hills and how she couldn't wait to get back there.'

'Moved out of there last summer. Bought themselves a derelict Victorian by the beach.' He glances to the ceiling. 'Teddy's supposed to be doing it up.'

Peter swaps his menu for a napkin. 'Great project. Bring

the old girl to life.' His eyes flick to June. 'Love to do it myself one day.' He raises a hand to summon a waitress.

June busies herself agreeing with Peter's choice of trout for her. He'll have steak, as ever.

The giving of food orders takes over, with Libby asking too many questions about the origins of the chicken and whether she can have beans, not peas. She can. Alf chooses roast lamb, with Peter expressing disappointment his guest doesn't want the lobster.

'Not fond of lobster, thanks, Peter. And this wasn't necessary because of the accident.' Alf wriggles in his seat, blushes faintly.

June would bet money he'll resist being paid for at the end of the evening. She skews the talk from Alf before Libby can attack with a thousand more intrusive questions.

'Tell us what Raine and Teddy are doing, apart from fixing up a house.' June sets her napkin on her lap. 'Is Teddy behaving himself?'

'Mostly.' Alf fiddles with his fork. 'He and Mr Greene, his dad, set up a cabinet-making business. Keeps Teddy's hands full, which is why the house is slow.'

'Are they happy? Raine and Teddy, I mean.' Libby leans forward, showing a generous hint of cleavage. 'It didn't look too good last time, not from what I could see.'

June's eyebrows arch at this bluntness. She wonders if she should call her friend on it. Maybe later, when the answers have been given.

'Yes, yes they are.' Alf's eyebrows match June's arch. 'Raine doesn't stand for any nonsense. Anyway, her own hands are full with her own business.' Pride gleams in his brown eyes.

'Really?' June is impressed, and Alf's pride is, well, interesting. She tucks away her feelings about that, for another time.

'Temporary secretarial staff, runs it with her sister.'

'Two women?' Peter's eyes widen. 'Do they have a good

accountant, a man to make sure the clients don't cheat them?'

June flushes at the arrogant comment. Alf has no chance to reply, should he want to, because their meals arrive and Peter's question can be safely ignored. The chat turns to talk of the Snowy scheme and what Alf might expect up there. Cold, wet, miserable, Libby asserts. Peter agrees, saying Alf should stay in Cooma, plenty of work.

'You'll have to come back often, find somewhere to warm up.' Libby waggles her pencilled brows. 'Or someone to warm up with.'

Alf glances up from cutting his potatoes, widened eyes accompanied by a small smile. 'You think?'

'Definitely.' Libby leaves it at that – a friendly challenge hanging there for Alf to take up.

June waits, not liking the pinch of sourness in her stomach. Libby's flirtatiousness is nothing new, and it isn't like June didn't expect it tonight. Yet it still annoys her. She's acting like a jealous teenager when she has no right, nor reason.

'Might be a good idea.' Alf's smile doesn't commit itself. 'Good food here. You enjoying your chicken, Libby?' And he returns to his lamb, leaving Libby with nowhere to go except talk about chicken.

Nicely done. June's sourness lightens, and the rest of the meal is spent discussing how fast Cooma is growing, how much construction work there is and how good it is for those in the trade.

Peter rests his arm across the back of June's chair and leans into her. She smells the wine on his breath as he nuzzles her hair before leaning away to smile at her. 'I'm a lucky man. This boom means we'll be pretty comfy in the long term, won't we, doll?'

June squirms at this casual use of 'we', and the phrase 'long-term'. She resists glancing Alf's way to see what he makes of it. Libby is exclaiming how lucky they are, and well deserved, two such wonderful people. She raises a glass and June takes the opportunity to wriggle out of Peter's embrace. Her face and throat are flushed.

'To future prosperity. And happiness.' Libby pushes her glass towards Alf, who responds with a soft, 'Hear, hear.'

June is grateful Libby didn't cheer 'the happy couple'.

In the subsequent round of clinking, she catches Alf's eye. He holds her look for a heartbeat before turning to tap glasses with Peter. June's pulse quickens, slows. The shadow of sadness is still there, the one she glimpsed three years ago. Sadness for what? Lost chances of happiness? Does Alf hanker for Raine? His gleam of pride. The polite brushing off of Libby's flirting.

June gives the same even smile to each of her dinner companions. 'To happiness.' Wherever it might be found. 'Anyone for sweets?'

◇◇◇◇◇

The night is clear, the stars as shiny as Alf has ever seen them. He's closer to the sky here in the mountains. It's cold, and he snuggles into his new, warm jacket, buttoned up to the neck.

He limps along, grateful for his stick steadying him on the damp footpath and for Libby's slow pace as she strolls beside him. The long woollen coat she wears over her dress adds to Alf's gratitude. He no longer has to keep his eyes fixed on her face to show they're not straying to the cleft between her breasts, which peeked out each time she leaned towards him during dinner. Libby is pretty, and sparkly, and flirtatious, and Alf enjoys her company and has no intention of taking her seriously. As Raine would say, with a sniff, she's likely the type to chase anything in trousers.

Whether that's the case or not, he's worried she's regretting her generosity in offering to walk him home after he refused Peter's offer to drive him. The boarding house is not far and Alf was already indebted. His host stymied his plan to pay his own way by sneaking to the bar to deal with the bill, instead of heading to the toilet as he said he was.

'It was kind of Peter to treat us all and to offer to drive.' He glances at Libby. 'Are you sure you'll be all right getting home yourself? I'm not much of a gentleman letting you walk *me* home.'

A cat darts out from a low hedge and across the road. Alf startles and Libby lets out a tiny shriek.

She giggles. 'Damn cat.'

She takes Alf's arm and steps closer. Her perfume is light, fruity, and pleasant, and Alf doesn't mind the closeness.

'Peter is a kind man.' Libby sighs. 'He's had his problems, but he has June now.'

She doesn't elaborate on the problems, and Alf doesn't ask. Everyone has problems. He can't help from probing about June, however, in an act of masochism akin to prodding a toothache.

'Peter and June seem happy. He dotes on her.' It's what's uppermost in Alf's mind from the evening: Peter's arm across June's shoulder, the pride of possession in his eyes, talking about 'we this', 'we that'.

'I introduced them.' Libby gives a skip, excited to be passing on her role in the romance. 'Rob, my big brother, threw a party for me for my last birthday and invited Peter along, try to shake him out of himself.' She snorts, delicately. 'I think he was trying to set us up. Only, Peter took one look at June and that was the end of that.'

'You don't mind?'

'Mind?' Libby giggles harder. 'Not my type. A little too, well, bossy for me. In a nice, protective way.' She gives Alf a cheeky look. 'I can look after myself, thank you.'

'I bet you can.' Alf would have bet money June could look after herself too, at least the June he once briefly knew.

'Peter's wife up and left him last year.' Libby pulls in her lips. 'All very sad. And June hadn't been out with anyone for ages and seemed happy that way. I had to bully her to get her there.' She tosses her head, grinning. 'Glad I did. They'll heal each other, and June will be a great mum to those tykes. I'm not mum material like she is.' Her grin softens. 'Yes, it's good for both of them.'

Alf's understanding that he's made a fool's journey deepens, if this was about picking up where he'd left off with June. How stupid could he be? What did he expect? For her to be waiting for him, when nothing had happened in three years bar a few sparse letters? He's his own worst enemy.

'I'm pleased for them.' If June is happy, Alf will be happy too.

Why is it then that he recalls her squirming out of Peter's embrace, her flushed face, the brief look she shared with him with its hint of awkwardness. A faint plea for help? No, he's reading too much into it, as usual. Walk away, leave it, lost cause.

They've reached the boarding house and stand by the gate in the white wooden fence. Libby chats brightly and Alf uh-uhs an automatic response.

'That's a yes?' She bats her eyelashes.

'Sorry, Libby, I was lost for a moment. What have I agreed to?'

'A film, and a coffee afterwards, tomorrow evening. I have a day shift, so it works well.'

He can't hide the surprise in his, 'Oh.'

She grins, touches his arm. 'I'm not proposing marriage, Alf. Merely a film and a chat.'

He guffaws, too energetically. 'Of course. If you don't mind being seen with a cripple, sounds good, thanks Libby.'

'Sorry to ask outright. Us nurses are known to be blunt, and you're here for such a short time, so I reckoned …'

'Yes, yes.' Alf is enthusiastic. He wants to go on this outing. He wants to spend time with this bubbly redhead, whatever her motivations. It sure beats an evening in the boarding house twiddling his thumbs. He worries about spending money he doesn't have, remembers he has a job for the time being and can afford it. Yes, he'll go and enjoy himself.

'Great!' Libby beams and opens the gate, ushering Alf through. 'You can manage from here?'

'Sure, thanks, Libby.'

'I'll collect you at seven, see you tomorrow.' She pulls the gate to and walks along the pavement, pausing once to turn and wave.

Alf waves. 'Go carefully!' He's enjoying himself, aching ankle or not. It's a nice change.

◇◇◇◇◇

'Why don't you come home with me tonight?' In the hotel dining room, Peter holds June's coat for her, waits for her to slip her arms into the sleeves and brushes her neck with his lips before releasing her.

'It's been a long day, a long week.' June wants to go to her own home, make herself a hot drink and curl up in bed with her library book. *East of Eden* demands close attention with its plethora of characters and will be a great escape for an hour before sleep.

She doesn't want to go to Peter's place, with all that entails, including dealing with Debbie and Ben come the morning. Whatever Peter says, June is certain his children don't adore her. Rather, she suspects they tolerate her as a stand-in until their missing mother returns. Her heart aches for them in an abstract way, not in any way which makes her want to mother them herself. Not yet. Perhaps it will change as her relationship with Peter deepens.

'Then what about something to drink at your place before I head off?'

'I'm sorry Peter, I'm exhausted and sleep calls. I'd be no fun at all, honest.' She gives him a coy look, trying to ease his disappointment.

'Fine.' He doesn't pout, remains the perfect gentleman. 'Let me take you home, unless you're going to insist on walking too?' He raises an eyebrow.

'No way.' She glances at her high heels. 'Not planning on a sprained ankle for myself.'

As they walk to the car, Peter takes June's arm and links it through his. 'I reckon Alf and Libby would make a great couple.' He turns to her. 'Like we make a great couple.'

June's tiredness is real, her emotions in a tangle over how she reacted this evening to Libby's flirting with Alf, and it comes out before she can think better of it.

'You forget, Peter. Technically, legally, you're already a couple, even if you've mislaid your wife.' She immediately regrets her tartness.

He stiffens but says nothing until they come to his car, where he leans against the side and pulls June into a close embrace before holding her at arm's length. 'The pavement isn't the best place to have this conversation, only I need to tell you I'm in the throes of divorcing Leah. The way it's happening, it shouldn't take long, and as soon as it's done I'll make an honest woman of you, June Lovell.'

June focuses on the practical question while she tries to deal with the implications of his statement. 'How can you divorce her when you don't have a clue where she is?'

'Ah, having no clue is what makes it easy. My solicitor tells me we have an interesting approach to divorce here, when one party can't be found.' He takes her face between his hands and peers into her eyes. Under the yellow gleam of the streetlight, they burn with an intensity June hasn't seen before. 'Leah's disappearing act can work in our favour, and I'll tell you why later, given how perishingly cold it is.'

He opens the passenger door, ushers June in and closes it before striding around to the driver's side. Through the fogged windscreen, June takes in his tall, upright form, the purposeful way he walks. A man in charge, a man who knows – and usually gets – what he wants. Life with Peter would be simple. She need never make another decision.

Is that what she wants?

Chapter Nine

WHEN ALF IS DROPPED OFF after work by Phil the next day, he finds Arthur in the boarding house sitting room, browsing through a three-day-old copy of *The Sydney Morning Herald*.

'About bloody time.' They chorus it and grin.

Alf limps forward to grasp Arthur's outstretched hand, wobbling dangerously. 'Good to see you at last, mate.'

Arthur grasps the hand more firmly. 'What the hell you been up to? Can't I leave you on your own for five bleeding minutes?'

The sofa takes Alf's hard slump into its worn cushions with a griping creak. 'Nothing serious, sprained my ankle first day on the job.' He dismisses the injury with a casual wave of the stick. 'It doesn't hurt anymore, just a nuisance getting around.' He grimaces. 'You got the note I left at The Royal?'

'Yeah, and sorry for taking so long to get here.' Arthur resumes his seat, setting the newspaper on a side table. 'I was out in one of the far camps and didn't see your letter 'til I got in to Adaminaby. Hitched a lift in a jeep, and thanks for the excuse to get out of there for a couple of days. Need the break.'

Alf plays host and hauls himself to his feet. 'Drink? Have you eaten?' He looks at his watch. 'Where you staying? You can probably bunk in with me if I clear it with Mrs Beale, the landlady. There's a second bed in my room.'

'Whoa, slow down and sit down.' Arthur pats the air and Alf sits like a well-trained dog. 'I met Mrs Beale, and we agreed I can stay a couple of nights. When I said I was here to take you up to the Scheme, she gave me a funny look.' He points to the ankle. 'No wonder. What's the plan? How long are you out of action? And what did you mean by saying you did your ankle in at work?'

Alf needs a beer before answering all these questions and sends Arthur to fetch one from the small stash in the bottom of his wardrobe. 'It'll be cool enough.'

A beer each in hand, Alf asks if Arthur has heard anything more about Mr Greene, and where does it leave him and Maggie with the wedding?

'We might have to put it off. All depends on how well Mr G recovers.' Arthur whooshes a long breath. 'Maggie's disappointed, we both are, but she can't leave while her dad's not earning. Her mum relies on her too much. And he'll need caring for when they let him out of hospital.'

'Handy to have a nurse for a daughter.'

Arthur sets his beer bottle on top of the newspaper. 'It wouldn't be so bad if Teddy didn't need Mr Greene's support for the cabinet-making. Raine's making barely enough to pay for the basics, and it's all a bit tight.'

'Yeah, she told me.' Alf says it absently, stifling his annoyance at Teddy's inability to come to grips with money as well as making beautiful furniture.

'Teddy's gotta pull his finger out.' Arthur's own frustration shows in his voice. He grabs the beer, takes a swallow. 'This should make him think harder about responsibilities, including that bloody great house he's supposedly doing up.'

There's a moment's silent staring at the brown carpet before Arthur lifts his head to gaze at Alf. 'Your turn. What's been happening to you in the short time you've been here?'

Alf tells the story of the delays in getting him up to the Scheme and the temporary work he's found while he waits for his ankle to improve and instructions on where to go, hoping the former is quicker than the latter. He's conscious of not mentioning June, which prods him into remembering he has a date of sorts with Libby.

'Damn, nearly forgot.' He looks at his watch. 'It's Mrs Beale's night off cooking, so I was planning on something at the café around the corner. Then I have to be here by seven, being collected for a date, of sorts.' He pulls in his lips. 'Sorry, pal, I'll have to leave you to fend for yourself, can't disappoint the lady.'

'A date?' Arthur's eyes gleam with curiosity. 'Nurse June? You tracked her down and you're going on a date?'

It takes work for Alf to not let disappointment colour his reply. 'No, not June. Another nurse, met her when I did my ankle in. Libby's her name. Redhead, fun, nothing serious of course. Not in such a short time.'

'Did you look June up?'

No, he didn't look her up. And it wouldn't have mattered if he had because–

'Yeah, saw her at the hospital. And, pure coincidence, it's her fiancé, boyfriend whatever' – he hasn't worked out which it is – 'I'm working for. Bigshot local house builder, doing well for himself. Lucky June.'

Arthur's eyebrows rise, and Alf worries he's let show the bitterness he's imprisoned deep in his gut. What's the point of bitterness when his sandcastles in the air proved to be exactly that?

'Ah.' Arthur stands, offers his hand to help Alf off the sofa. 'Disappointing. I seriously had the impression she asked after you with a hint of something special. Like, properly interested to know.'

Alf props himself on his stick. 'Why would she be? Look at what she has! I'm a jobless, wandering sparky, hardly competition.' He hauls his emotions back to where they should be. 'Supposing I wanted her to be interested, of course.'

'Yeah.' Arthur's voice is unconvincing.

Alf limps to the door. 'Let's go eat, I'm starving.'

⸻

'Went to see a film last night.'

They're the first words out of Libby's mouth when June walks into the muggy warmth of the nurses' staff room.

Her friend's bantering tone tells June there's more to this than a film outing. The image pops into her head of Libby leading Alf out of the hotel after the dinner, her re-lipsticked mouth laughing, the solicitous way she touched his arm, and how she slowed her walk to match his limp. June will play it casual.

'Oh, what film did you see?'

'*Roman Holiday*.' Libby collects a second cup and saucer from a cupboard and sets them on the table before returning to hover over the kettle. 'Such a sad film. I mean, just because she's a princess, why can't she fall in love with Gregory Peck?'

'Uh huh.' When June saw the film with Peter, she'd found it sad too, despite its comedy billing. Princess Anna's lack of choice, how her path was set and duty dictated her future, had touched June in a personal way. She is no princess, yet, like Anna, her path could set like concrete around her if she lets Peter have his way.

Libby's chatter comes into focus when June hears Alf's name. Ah, she was spot on.

'Are you listening to me, June Lovell? Do you want this tea I'm making for you?'

'Sorry, Libby, yes, great film. Adore Hepburn, gorgeous and a great actress.' She rolls her eyes. 'Some women have it all.'

'Did you hear me say I went with Alf? And afterwards to the new Italian espresso bar in Sharpe Street for cappuccinos.'

The door opens and Stella bursts through, makes a beeline for the sofa and slumps into it.

'Aahhh! So good! Been on my feet six hours without a break.' She leans back and closes her eyes.

'Poor you. That'll be me in a few hours.' June fetches another cup to revive her colleague. On the way, she goes back to her and Libby's conversation.

'Nice about the espresso bar.' June conjures it. 'Peter refuses to go, mutters about new-fangled fancy drinks and what's wrong with coffee made in a pot?' She laughs, covering the spike of jealousy at the picture of Libby and Alf in earnest conversation in the tiny café with its candlewax-streaked bottles she's glimpsed through the window.

'Alf is sweet.' Libby clasps her hands to her chest, lifts her eyes to the ceiling. 'I could absolutely fall for him. He's so, so … attentive. You sense he'd always have your back, be there for you.' She squints at June. 'You know what I mean?'

June sits to pour the tea. 'He was the same with Raine, the woman who had the baby early. Protective as a bulldog, even with her husband.'

'Hmm.' Libby blows on the hot drink. 'He must be over her, surely?'

'Don't bank on it.' The darkness in Alf's eyes carries meaning. A warning? 'Don't forget he's leaving soon. Not a good idea to fall in love with an absentee.'

'I'll write.' Libby is confident. 'Lots of girls write, keep their relationships going at a distance. After all –' she giggles '– not a lot of competition up there and not much else to do.'

'I wouldn't bank on that either. Alf isn't good at letters.' It comes out more tartly than it should, and June flushes.

Stella opens her eyes, stretches and leans forward, elbows planted on her knees. 'You wrote to him? Remember, I was around then, enjoying the whole spectacle from a safe distance.' She touches a finger to her lips, pouts. 'You sly thing, you never let on.'

June shrugs, pretends nonchalance. 'Not for long. I guess we ran out of things to say.'

Or Alf ran out of things to say. She'd taken the hint, moved on. It wasn't like they'd spent days and nights in each other's arms in a torrid affair. A friendship born of circumstances, and when those circumstances changed, the friendship withered like a shallow-rooted vine.

Stella doesn't let it go. 'Do you fancy him? Is that why you're heading poor Libby off like a runaway steer?' She's moved to the table to collect her hot drink and stands close to June, staring into her face.

June doesn't blink, opens her mouth to protest, and grows hotter under Stella's frank gaze.

Libby cuts in. 'Of course she doesn't fancy him.' She's strident. 'She has Peter, and what more would a girl want? Looks, money, nice house, readymade family. Perfect.'

'I wonder.' Stella returns to the sofa. 'I wondered at the time, if there might be something between the two of you. Then he left and nothing happened. Now he's here. Hmm.'

This catty stirring isn't normal for Stella. It's exhaustion. The woman needs a good sleep.

'Tell me it's not true?' Libby's stridency remains. 'You can't be greedy, June, and hog all the best men.'

June backpedals. 'I was trying to be a friend, to look out for you, but if you're set on this, here's my advice.' She leans across to grasp Libby's hands. 'Write every day, beg him to write too, and I'll dance at your wedding with an excess of joy. I mean it, cross my heart.'

She lets go of Libby's hands. 'And now I have to find out what mayhem the new young doctor is wreaking out there.'

⋄⋄⋄⋄⋄

The new young doctor wreaks no havoc, and June's shift finishes when it's meant to. There's no one in the nurses' room when she fetches her coat, hat and gloves, for which she's grateful. She doesn't want to go over the who has whom debate, like a bunch of hormone-fired schoolgirls. She walks home in the late night, tightening her coat over her uniform and treading warily around icy patches formed by melting snow and a cloudless, star-brilliant sky. There are few people on the streets and even fewer lights shining in the windows of the houses along her route. The quiet is welcome after the coughs and stirrings of night-time wards.

At home, she makes cocoa and slouches on the sofa listening to a blues program on the wireless, urging the quiet of the outside to calm her own troubled thoughts.

Does she have Peter, as Libby insists? What about Peter's

wife? After dinner last night, when the kids were playing in Ben's room, he'd explained his ambiguous comment about Leah's disappearance and how it would 'help them'. It seems the law allows him to write to her, pleading for her return. If Leah doesn't respond, she'll be deemed guilty of desertion, and Peter can file for divorce immediately.

'You don't have any idea where she is.'

'Exactly. The solicitor said to post it to someone who might have an idea, although I drew a blank on that front when she left.' He crossed his arms and leaned back in the chair. 'Not one of them had a clue, yeah.' His bitterness touched her.

'Are you going to do it?'

'Done, yesterday.' He uncrossed his arms, raised his palms. 'Now we wait. I doubt if the letter will find her.' He gave her his best smile. 'And we can move on, as we want to.'

A niggling sense of discomfort about the one-sided nature of the process makes it hard for June to return Peter's enthusiasm. And there's the bitterness, suggesting Peter isn't altogether happy Leah is out of his, and the kids', lives.

Another niggle worms its way to sit beside this one. Would she have been gladder of this news a week ago, before Alf turning up here?

She finishes the cocoa, struggles off the sofa and stretches, the hand not holding the mug rubbing her aching back.

Why does she have to make this complicated? The facts are simple: Alf is not interested in her, and, if Libby has her persuasive way, will never be. Whatever spark lit three years ago has died of malnourishment. On the other hand, the great catch, Peter, loves her and wants her to be his wife. Peter is kind, attentive, a good father. She can easily return his love if she allows herself to not worry about runaway wives. He'll get his divorce and they can move forward together, like he said. It's neat, tidy. Too neat?

Rinsing the mug in the sink, peering into the dark garden beyond the window, neat and tidy appears attractive, restful. She makes a decision. Tomorrow she'll buy Debbie the frilly net petticoat she saw in Mrs Elbra's window.

Chapter Ten

THE SECRETARY LOOKS UP FROM her typing. She gives Alf a crisp nod and a tip of her head towards Peter's open office door.

'He's in, go ahead.'

A bright late morning sun through the window highlights dancing dust motes and helps warm the otherwise cool room. An electric radiator sits in a corner, its elements grey with cold. Alf is glad he kept his coat on. When he hovers in the doorway, Peter, dressed in a bulky jumper, pushes aside the plans he's poring over.

'Come in, come in. What's the news?'

'Off to Jindabyne tomorrow.' Alf sits in the visitor's chair and rests his stick across his knees.

Peter peers over his desk, shaking his head. 'You sure the ankle's up to it?'

Alf glances down. 'When I told them about it, they said come on up anyway, they can give me light work in Jindy until it heals properly.' He gives the ankle a tentative twist. Not too painful. 'Not much choice I guess.'

'Hmm. Tomorrow. So soon?'

'Snow's passable, and my mate Arthur, who was supposed to meet me here when I first arrived, well, he's off to Adaminaby this afternoon. No reason to hang about.'

'I wish you'd reconsider.' Peter pushes back his chair. 'Could do with you staying on here with all the work.' He leans forward, benign. 'And June enjoyed our dinner the other night. We could have you over to the house sometime. Meet the kids too.'

Alf crosses and uncrosses his legs, imagining the domesticity of the proposed evening. A repeat of the many evenings he's spent at Raine and Teddy's, which are, let's face it, a good chunk of the reason he's travelled all this way to find a different reality.

'Ah, thanks, sounds good, but no time now.' He's

apologetic, hoping to convey polite interest if not enthusiasm.

Peter is oblivious. 'And Libby too.' He winks. 'A terrific girl, Libby, plenty of life in her, deserves a good fella.'

Libby? She must have talked to June about their evening out. A film and a coffee. Nothing to warrant winks.

'Uh huh. Yeah, perhaps another day.'

'Of course, you'll visit from time to time.'

Alf assesses Peter's self-assured manner. What must it be like to be comfortable in your own skin, to understand your place in the world and be happy about it? He pulls himself upright.

'Won't keep you any longer, just came by to let you know my plans.'

'Sure, of course, and I'll make sure your pay packet is made up if you want to come by early tomorrow and collect it.'

'Thanks, appreciate it.' It means Alf doesn't have to draw on his savings to settle his boarding house bill and pay his bus fare to Jindabyne.

Peter walks around to shake Alf's hand, wishes him all the best, he'll see him soon and be careful up there, and Alf is free to leave. He sends his regards to June on his way out, nods at the secretary, pulls his hat from his pocket, stuffs it on his head and limps awkwardly outside.

As if summoned by mention of her name, June is approaching the office along the gravelled walkway from the footpath. Her head is down, eyeing a beribboned, pink paper parcel in her hands. When she sees Alf she stops, eyes startled, before dragging out a smile and walking forward.

'Hi, Alf. Didn't expect to see you here.'

'Came to tell the boss I'm off to Jindabyne tomorrow.' He runs out of words. There's an awkwardness, a hesitancy, about June's manner which wasn't there in the hospital, or at the dinner. What's happened? Nothing he's done, he hasn't seen her.

June clears her throat, gazes at the white gravel as if drawing courage, or inspiration, from its cold stoniness. She lifts her head. 'Libby will be sorry to see you go.' She holds his gaze.

Libby again? They met a few days ago. It's hardly a relationship.

'You think so, given we've only met a couple of times? She's a nice woman.' He flinches inwardly at the banality.

June's eyes widen. 'She'll miss you.' Her intensity as she stares at him makes Alf want to step away. 'She likes you, a lot, and she's going to write to you.' Her voice is taut, with a tremor as if she wanted to make a different point, but this is the one she's embarked on and she'll see it through. 'You will write back this time, won't you?'

The stab of guilt hurts. Alf's jacket is suddenly too warm and he's babbling.

'I'm sorry. About the letters, I mean. Your letters. I loved getting them, I missed you, how kind you were to me, to us …' He swallows. 'I wanted to write …'

She tips her head to the side, inviting explanation.

'…only, what did I have to write about? Building houses and hanging out with Teddy and Raine.' His ankle aches, out in the cold like this. He rests more heavily on the stick, fearful of falling at June's feet like a remorseful penitent. Yet he has no wish to leave, to put an end to being here with her. He wants to be here, wherever it takes him.

'I understand.'

Does she? Alf doubts it. Or worries that what she understands isn't the right version of what there is to be understood.

'I was hurt, it's true.' Her gaze returns to the stones and she squeezes the gift-wrapped package. 'And then I thought –' the intent scrutiny returns – 'he's not over Raine.'

Alf's heart thuds too loudly at this frontal assault. He wants to protest, to deny. June's stare dares him.

'I … I –'

'It's okay.'

Her tenderness, shadowed with sorrow, brings pricking tears. Alf blinks, takes his own gaze to the spot on the ground June abandoned a moment ago.

'You're the sweetest person, Alf, and any woman with an ounce of sense would want you for her own.'

Is she talking about herself? He tries to read her tone. The sorrow remains and now the shadows are of, what? Resignation?

'And to be fair on that woman, you have to want her as much as – even more than – she wants you. Deep inside you, truly need and love her.'

A boulder-like weight settles in Alf's gut. The gravelled footpath is an unlikely setting for a conversation about love. It could be one June has had with herself and has to spill it out while there's an audience who might be sympathetic. His brain is in chaos, emotions tumbling like flailing acrobats. There's nothing he can say. He stands there, exposed and vulnerable, yet safe in June's gentle sympathy.

'I don't know what to say.' It's pathetic, and true.

She tucks the parcel under one arm and touches her gloved hand to his face. The look they share sears Alf's soul. He blinks first.

'Don't say anything.' Her smile is real. 'Remember how we talked once about Teddy, and I said he'd done the right thing to flee to the mountains because they'll clear your head?'

'Yes.'

'Go to the mountains, Alf, clear your head. And try not to hurt Libby.' Her voice lightens, ripples with soft laughter. 'She's outrageous and a flirt, with deeper feelings than she lets on.'

'No, yes, of course.' He's bumbling again.

June stares past him to the door of Peter's office. She turns the parcel in her hands as if it contains the answer to life's mysteries, if only she can find the key to open it.

'Remembered something I forgot to do.' June wheels around, walks along the gravel, boots crunching, calling over her shoulder. 'Make the most of the mountains, Alf. Work it out.'

Does Alf really hear the murmured 'Please' which follows?

His mind continues its turmoil as he shuffles along the footpath. Was the conversation, one-sided as it was, all about him? Why the sorrow, the resignation in June's voice, her eyes, her touch? He aches to drive it all away, except … it's not his place. Never has been. June has Peter to drive out whatever sadness holds her.

When Alf reaches the café where he's to meet Arthur for lunch, he finds him sitting with Libby, her hands wrapped around a Coke. However she's arrived here, he's glad, as he can say goodbye without deliberately seeking her out, something she might read more into than is meant.

'Here he is.' Arthur shifts his chair along, the chrome legs scraping the wooden floor, to create a wider gap for Alf and his stick.

The café is crowded with women, mostly, in pairs and groups, shopping bags at their feet, chatting loudly, laughing, pouring teas and eating sandwiches and salads. The windows are misted on the inside, the air smells of toasted cheese.

Alf sits heavily, glad to have the weight off his aching ankle. 'You two have met?'

Libby came looking for Alf at the boarding house after her shift, and Arthur overheard her questioning the landlady about his whereabouts.

Over ham sandwiches, Arthur apologises for his lack of usefulness during his short visit. 'You didn't need me after all.' He thumps Alf on the shoulder, causing him to splutter. 'Sorted yourself out, haven't you, mate?' He eyes Libby with approval. 'And very nicely too.'

The café's warmth turns to hot stuffiness.

Libby grins. 'Everyone wants to look after you, Alf.' She strokes his hand. 'Brings out the best in us.'

Her fingers, cool from the Coke, dance lightly on his skin. Alf finds the sensation pleasant.

Arthur stands. 'I need to move, fetch my bag and head off to the bus station.' He nods at Libby. 'Great to meet you and hope to see you soon.' He clasps Alf's shoulder. 'See you soon, mate. You know where to find me if you need me.'

He pats his pockets and leaves a few coins on the table. Alf's protests are ignored, and Arthur wanders to the door. He turns, and over the heads of the chatting groups of women, gives a thumbs up to Alf before walking into the street.

'Nice man.' Libby pushes aside her plate. 'Girlfriend? Wife?'

'Maggie. She's a nurse too.' Alf huffs. 'They've been together forever, engaged and everything. Arthur has this fixation about having to buy their own home before they get married, which is why he's here.'

'And Maggie? What does she think?'

'She'd rather be married, with a kid or two.'

'Ah. Well, I hope it happens soon for them.' Libby gives a coy bat of her eyes. 'The path of true love, hey?'

'Yeah.'

She twists her fingers together, clears her throat. 'I don't want you to think I'm pushy and forward.' A sly smile. 'And I guess we've hardly met, but I like you, Alf, and I'd love it if we could write, and if you visited from time to time to say hi.'

Two bright pink spots bloom on her cheeks. Alf is touched. Libby's not as brazen as she pretends, and what can he say to this request except –

'Yes, of course. I could do with good friends here if I end up staying.'

Libby untwines her fingers to give a little clap. 'Good!'

Later, when Alf is packing, he thinks about this commitment he's made to keep in touch. It's an act of friendship, that's all. He experiences a guilty twinge because he suspects it's not how Libby sees it. He pauses in the middle of folding a jumper because it's not Libby he's imagining.

There was more than sympathy in the look he and June shared earlier on the cold gravel path. There was a wistfulness in her eyes. He wishes he knew the thoughts, emotions, behind the wistfulness. If he tried hard, he could kid himself the aura of loss June carries might be about him.

Now he is leaving, Alf finally gives in to the memories of their last meeting nearly three years ago.

October had finally quashed the late seasonal snow when June led Alf up the track to a lookout above the town with a view to the mountains, sculptured shapes dark against a brilliant blue sky. They sat side by side on a rock, June pointing out a handful of landmarks below and the names of one or two of the higher mountains.

'June –'

She turned to him, her eyes the same colour and brightness of the sky, her mouth partly open in a soft smile.

'I want to say …' Whatever he wanted to say was distracted by her lips. He fought on. 'To say thank you, for everything you've done for us. For Raine, Teddy, me.'

Especially him. Raine's forgiveness of Teddy, his genuine repentance, how the two appeared closer than they had been before all this; the tenderness with which Teddy cradled his baby daughter; and the love in Raine's eyes as she watched them … All this split Alf's heart in two.

He was happy for his best friend, of course he was. And whatever made Raine happy, made Alf happy too. Of course it did. He had lost, and he had to let go his feelings for her, or at least bury them in a pit so deep they could never clamber out.

June's kindness, her quiet sympathy, had eased his struggles. His gratitude was enormous, and would, he believed, last forever.

June's smile had turned tender. She laid a cool palm on Alf's cheek. 'For you, Alf. Don't you see? I've done it for you.' She kept her eyes on his, willing him to understand.

Alf's breath caught. He reached up his own hands to cup her cheeks, bent towards her. The kiss was long, sweet. Alf pulled away first. He stood, on legs which shook, and turned to face the mountains. Not now, not yet.

'I don't know what to –'

June, sitting on the rock, reached out a hand to touch his arm. 'It's okay, Alf. I understand.'

'I'm sorry.' He faced her, distressed to see her eyes moist with tears, the smile gone.

'Don't be sorry. I shouldn't have done that.' She gave him a tremulous grin. 'Let's stay in touch, hey? Let's be friends.'

In his room in the boarding house, Alf refolds the jumper, which he's scrunched into a ball, and places it carefully in his case. Is it his imagination, or does June lack the joyful bubbliness he'd expect in a recently happily engaged woman? Could it be she regrets things too? No … Look what she has.

He shouldn't have come here, stirred up emotions he could do nothing about. Damn Arthur and his teasing. He's glad he's leaving. His visits will be rare and short.

◇◇◇◇◇

The pink parcel weighs heavily in June's hands, despite its featherweight contents of a rainbow petticoat. Her way forward had been clear, last night. Bumping into Alf means everything's a tangle again. She lifts her head to take in the mountains filling the bright blue sky at the end of Sharpe Street.

What did she say to Alf? About how he has to want a woman as much, more perhaps, than the woman wants him. Truly need and love her. She should turn those words on herself. Is Peter the man she needs and loves?

Go to the mountains to clear your head, Alf. Good advice. She should take it herself. The mountains aren't possible today, but there is a place she can go. She turns on her heel, excuses herself to the man in the heavy overcoat whom she runs into, and walks to Massie Street, where she follows the uphill path to Nanny Goat Hill. The narrow track is bordered with slush which seeps across the icy ground, puddling in dips and cracks. June, in her boots, is impervious to wet and keeps up her rapid stride to the lookout. She needs perspective.

With her back to the pile of rocks, and the parcel pressed into a ledge, she stares over the outer remnants of the town to where the white humps of the mountains curve above the plain. When her head doesn't immediately clear, she lowers her gaze. The home she knows so well lies below her, cars travelling through its criss-cross of streets, distant people hurrying along wide footpaths to disappear under shop verandahs and re-appear as if pulled from a magician's hat. She breathes in the frosty air, closes her eyes and challenges the winter sun to warm her face.

What rises in her mind is the look she shared with Alf. Loss, sadness, wanting the unattainable yet unable to strive for it because the shape of life forbids it. Her own part in this sharing, right by Peter's office, might have been a betrayal of some sort. As is her memory of the kiss she and Alf shared here that bright October day.

Her stomach roils thinking over her words just now to Alf. Accusing him straight out of being in love with Raine, of holding a futile candle for a married woman with two kids. Alf's blushing reaction suggests the accusation hit home.

Is Libby the person to sever this romantic thread, given it must be stretched and frayed by now? Could be. She imagines the two of them together, the night of the hotel dinner, and recalls Libby's words about being serious this time. Libby is never serious about the men who briefly inhabit her life. She finds their attentions shallow, which, June has pointed out, is no great surprise given the way she acts – all flirtatious eyes and pretend coyness. Libby had shrugged at this, saying she would know the right man when he came along and she'd be her real self for him.

Alf and Libby. June opens her eyes and tugs her coat more tightly about her. The wind is colder, stronger on the exposed lookout than in the sheltered streets.

Libby and Alf. She'll work hard to be glad for them if it works out. She will dance at their wedding, as she promised. Meanwhile, the frilly petticoat can remain ungiven. Until her own heart fully declares itself, one way or the other.

Chapter Eleven

WINTER MORPHS INTO SPRING. ALF is captive to the beauty of snow-laden eucalypts emerging into sunlight, and rocks exposing their grey granite surfaces to the balmier air. The newness of it all dulls, however, overwhelmed by the reality of sleeping under canvas on a camp bed two feet from a snoring tent-mate, showering in a freezing wooden hut, and never being alone. The camaraderie of the camp hasn't yielded him a close friend. Alf is too used to being the one apart, the one not a couple, to making do with his own company and his music. He misses his music, misses Teddy's grumbles, Maggie's teasing and his confiding chats with Raine.

He empathises with Teddy's months in Guthega and raises Arthur to god-like status for having lived and worked like this for so long. Luckily for Arthur, he's not often in the camps these days, having made his way up the Authority ladder to a cushy job in a real office in Adaminaby. He talks about staying on, bringing Maggie up, settle in Cooma where Maggie could work at the hospital. With Libby and June. Libby and Maggie would get on like a house on fire. What would Maggie make of June?

This clear, chill morning, as on most mornings, Alf is carted off to a new section of tunnel where he and other electricians are needed. Their transport is a wooden-sided open tram with a stretched canvas roof, a land-bound version of Popeye, the pleasure boats on the river at home. He's crammed in with fellow workers chattering in a dozen languages.

While they clatter along the metal track, Alf's thoughts return to yesterday's trip into Jindabyne. He'd hitched a lift in a Land Rover driven through the slush by a careful German, and treated himself to lunch at the old hotel. The deep chair where Raine and her pregnant belly curled the afternoon and evening they waited for news of Teddy is there, by the fire. Alf avoided sitting in it. The hen-breasted landlady is also there, pragmatic and friendly. She didn't recognise Alf, and why should she? Hundreds of workers and dozens of dramas have doubtless passed through her hotel since then.

Their own drama plays in his mind like the memory of a film – events which happened to other people, experienced second-hand on a big screen.

The tram arrives at the work site, the workers scramble down with their kit and the electricians gather to find out what today's job is.

The foreman is dwarfed by a steep slope of quarried-out rocks behind him, above which a massive triple-arched steel girder holds a new tunnel in place.

'Cables.' The foreman waves his arm towards the roof. 'Up there. You all know what to do.'

Alf's stomach clenches. Last week they strung electric lines above temporary rail tracks to carry men and equipment into the tunnels being carved from the mountains' guts. Relatively easy work. Today, he'll have to clamber up those uneven, squared-off rocks to lay thick, heavy steel cables below the girder, along the tunnel's roof.

He peers at his colleagues. If any of them are fazed by the challenge, they hide it well. The first to shoulder his bag and start the climb is a man whom the other electricians praise for his fearless approach. Foolish is the word Alf would use. The fellow, Sam, is a Korean vet who returned from the war physically unscathed and, in Alf's view, mentally raddled. Alf worries for him, sees him taking too many risks. So far, the blighter's been lucky.

Alf follows, using ropes dangling from the steel beams above to steady himself. Not good with heights, he concentrates on the rock face and what he has to do. He's thankful for his sturdy boots – bought on an earlier trip to Jindabyne on the advice of a fellow sparky – and glad too for his hard hat. Stupidly peering into the depths from a narrow ledge near the tunnel roof, he isn't sure what good the hat will do if he takes a tumble. Nausea rises up his throat, imagining his body bouncing from rock to rock to the boulder-strewn floor.

'You don't like it up here, do you, Alf?' It's Sam, squeezed shoulder-to-shoulder with Alf on the ledge. His question is neutral, he's not being unkind.

'Not my idea of fun, no.'

Sam grunts, hauls himself to the next perch and offers his hand to help Alf up. Alf hesitates before taking it. The crazed glint in Sam's eyes doesn't encourage him to accept the offer.

'Don't be an idiot.' Sam pushes his arm lower. Alf takes a breath, grabs the offered hand and uses his feet to get purchase as Sam hauls.

He has no time to say thanks before Sam releases him and sidles along to where three others are inspecting a cable and eyeing the rock wall to determine how to set the cable in place. Alf joins them. It's going to be a long day.

Later, as the sun falls behind the mountains, Alf lies on his camp bed, hands under his head, staring at the stains in the canvas roof. He needs to shower, eat, and sleep, but first he needs to think about Raine's letter, and what he should do about it.

Mr G is doing well, though he won't go back to fulltime work. He's near enough to retirement that the Housing Trust have said they can work something out. When he's fit enough, he'll help Teddy in the business, if the business is still going (heavily underscored). *It's hopeless. Teddy won't see he can't take as long as he does on pieces. Even the customers complain about the wait! Whenever I try talking to him, we end up fighting. I wish you were here, Alf. You might be able to talk sense into his bull-headed brain.*

Alf's ability to talk sense into Teddy has been tested in the past, and, frankly, found wanting. What Raine is asking for is moral support, which has also been tested in the past and, in this case, comes up trumps. It's why Alf's always been a 'terrific friend'. He snorts, realising he's not desperate to rush home to let Raine cry on his shoulder. It's a mess, a typical Teddy mess. Teddy is the one who has to fix it, and Alf's haranguing won't make that happen. The business going under might be the shock treatment his obstinate friend needs to jolt some sense into his head, force him into working differently. If there is a complete meltdown, Alf will go home, for Raine's sake.

'A good day, Alf?'

His tent mate has returned from the shower, wet towel over his shoulder, hair slicked to his scalp. He pegs the towel to a string attached to the roof pole, tosses his dirty clothes onto a stool, ready to wear tomorrow.

'Yeah, if you call death-defying rock-climbing a good day.'

The man, a burly Australian, chuckles. He's a carpenter, building temporary bridges ahead of proper roads being laid. He's been here six months and maintains he'll last a year, then he's off. Except for the snoring, Alf could have worse tent-fellows.

'Good. See you at dinner.' He pushes open the flaps, peers over his shoulder. 'Whatever's in the letter, mate, hope it's not all bad news.' And disappears into the near dark.

Does Alf look so sombre? Possibly. Because while he's decided to delay a return home, he has to answer a more urgent question, one he's avoided for too long. Does he want to make a much shorter journey and visit Cooma? It means seeing Libby, because what other reason does he have to go there?

He rolls onto his stomach and reaches under the camp bed where Libby's letters lie in a biscuit tin begged from the kitchens. He taps the tin, doesn't pull it out, and rolls onto his back.

Libby writes regularly, her letters filled with funny hospital happenings, films she's seen, and musings on life. Alf writes enough to be polite, he hopes. It's not been difficult, given he hasn't much going on and a whole new way of life for the telling. Occasionally, Libby mentions June, and Peter. It might be a 'June says hello' or it might be about spending an evening with them and how good they are together.

Good together. Alf wishes the spike of hurt the phrase causes would bugger off.

He hauls himself off the bed, grabs his towel and washbag and plods to the cold shower shed. The mountains loom on all sides of the camp, and Alf thinks of June's promise that if he let them, they would clear his head. Her promise has been fulfilled, Alf believes. Without bringing comfort.

In his ample thinking time, he's finally admitted June was the reason he returned. If it was all to do with a change of scenery, of flying solo instead of behind Raine and Teddy's V formation, he could have gone anywhere. Hell, he needn't have left the state. It was Arthur's fault, saying what he said about June asking after him. That's when Alf gathered up the sand of his memories and piled it into castles. Castles in the air as it's turned out.

Hope there is dead. And while Libby is fun and pretty, Alf feels nothing for her except a vague friendship. So what keeps him here in cold and danger, apart from an unwillingness to be seen throwing in the towel too early? He imagines the mockery. Teddy lasted longer than this, and had the excuse of his too-close brush with death to leave permanently.

He should throw it in, pass through Cooma on his way home, say hello to Libby and hope it's all he needs to say, and go back to being Raine's terrific friend. There's an icy weight in his stomach which no way forward he can think of will melt. He reaches the shed and steels himself for a shower as lukewarm as his enthusiasm for the future.

◇◇◇◇◇

It's September, and Peter's letter to Leah begging for her return to the marital home remains unanswered.

'How long has she got?' June lifts her after-dinner coffee from the restaurant table's white cloth and speaks before taking a sip of the scalding liquid. She is ambivalent about the answer. In this hiatus, there's no need to make decisions.

Peter pulls a packet of cigarettes from his jacket pocket, taps one out, clamps it between his lips and digs for matches. It's a new habit which June tries to discourage.

'Not sure, not much longer, I think.' He strikes a match and touches it to the end of the cigarette. 'Seeing the solicitor later this week to sort it out.' He grins, ebullient. 'Can't be too much longer to wait, and then we'll have a party to celebrate our engagement.' He raises his beer in a salute.

It's a statement. June racks her brains for memories of the occasion Peter proposed. To no avail. Her answer of 'yes' is similarly elusive. As is any clarity about what her answer would be if actually asked. She should say something, make sure Peter understands she's not committed. It doesn't mean she never will be. She needs more time, and it's premature to think of engagement parties.

'Peter, I think –'

'We'll have it at home. Hire one of those fancy marquees for the garden, invite the town. Have a real blowout.' His face fills with laughter lines. His eyes are bright.

It's an attractive, warm face. June falters, distracted, ploughs on.

'There's something –'

'Which reminds me, I've been meaning to tell you I'm thinking of buying one of those old houses near Sharpe Street, like the one your flat's in.' He leans towards her, suddenly deadpan. 'Might buy your place.'

The distraction is complete. 'What? Why?' Is he planning on driving her out of her home to force her to live with him and the kids?

'Joking, doll, joking.' He strokes her arm, drags on the cigarette. 'A house like it is what I mean, to do up, be our place.' He squints at her through smoke. 'Or would you prefer a new house? Build it as you want it, no cookie cut-out.'

June's brain spins. Old houses, new houses, engagement parties, marquees … She draws in a breath, clutches the coffee cup in two hands.

'Isn't it too early to be planning all this? I mean, I'm flattered, I love old houses, only …' She pulls in her lips, releases them with the barest smack. 'There's a divorce to go through and a lot to worry about –'

His frown is fleeting, replaced by a beam. 'You're right. I get carried away. One thing at a time – party plan!'

June shakes her head, and Peter takes this as playful agreement. 'Libby'll have to persuade Alf here for the occasion. They're still an item, aren't they?'

The abrupt switch is a relief. This is safer, if not more comfortable, territory, and June reaches for the lifebuoy.

'Libby thinks so.' She sets the coffee in its saucer. 'She writes, and Alf returns the favour.'

Yesterday, another ripped-open envelope lay on the table in the nurses' staff room when June arrived. She hung her cape on a hook, calling good morning. Libby, hovering over the kettle, had grinned and jerked her head at the letter.

'Two in two weeks.' She smirked. 'Do you finally believe me when I told you Alf would write?'

June covered her old hurt with a laugh. 'Obviously you have the touch. What does he have to say this time?'

Libby reads June bits of these missives – anecdotes about funny misunderstandings between the camp's inhabitants when broken English is the common language; or the evenings when men from all over Europe tell ancient folktales and sing mystical songs around the fire. June is as eager to hear these stories as Libby is to tell them. Libby never reads, or alludes to, anything personal. Either personal doesn't exist or Libby holds these parts close.

Either way, June is conflicted. Should she worry for her

friend, ask outright if this correspondence is blossoming into a romantic relationship? Or should she indulge the spark of hope that refuses to die, that the hint of loss in Alf's eyes, the unspoken intimacy of their rare shared glances, could be about her? She silently rebukes herself. She's as industrious as Libby when it comes to spinning webs from nothing.

'They write to each other. Is that it?' Peter's cigarette is a glowing stub which he crushes into the heavy glass ashtray.

A waitress asks if they want anything else, and Peter says the bill, please. When she leaves, he turns to June. 'No real gossip? Love in the air?'

'No.' June smiles to hide her brusqueness. 'But his last letter said he's thinking of coming to Cooma, I suppose for a break. We'll see then what the state of play is.'

June isn't sure she wants to know.

Chapter Twelve

THE KOOKABURRA WAKES ALF NOT five minutes after he's finally fallen asleep in his bed at the Old Jindabyne Hotel. The bed is too comfortable after the camp, and solid walls protecting him from the steady drizzling rain make him claustrophobic. He sits up, leans against the dark wood bedhead and lets his mind and body wake.

His suitcase lies open on the floor, all his worldly possessions contained therein. His wallet is stuffed with pound notes and coins. His savings book records the worth of his labour in the tunnels.

And what will he spend this bounty on? The best he can come up with is an overnight sleeper train from Melbourne to home rather than a cramped bus.

His decision to abandon the camp came easily in the end. One harrowing day too many, and a badly injured fellow sparky. His worries for the risk-taking Sam, the Korean veteran, proved prophetic. The man will live, with his body as raddled as his mind for the rest of his life. It was the prod Alf needed. Although, now he's here, on his way, he's having second thoughts.

What's he going to? How far will he go? To Cooma? Melbourne? All the way home or somewhere else altogether?

He's anxious about seeing Libby, which he has to do, for her sake and his. Her letters have brought him cheer, have been the brightest light these past couple of months. Who knows what possibilities that might yield? When he's face to face with her, lights might glitter and cooing doves might appear above her head, like a Disney fantasy. And life will be sorted.

He rubs his eyes, unable to believe in this vision. He shouldn't have left the camp. He should look out a ride back, return to stringing cables and climbing rocks. Let the world beyond take care of itself.

A return to boredom and loneliness.

No.

He swings his legs out of the warm bed, bare feet on the cold floor, and tells himself not to be pathetic. He'll go home, see his mates, who will gather him to their collective breast where he can be as content as he was before. With a fuller bank account.

Bacon, eggs and fried bread help his mood. Spring sunshine too. He takes deep breaths of the balmy early morning and boards the bus to Cooma with a sense of relief at having taken a positive step. His handful of fellow passengers are all men, all of them travelling alone. They nod politely and find seats which Alf would bet were equidistant from each other.

The creaky vehicle sways around rutted bends, groans its uphill efforts, wheels juddering in and out of potholes. Alf sways too, dozes, and startles awake at a particularly vicious bump. His hand goes to the top of the seat in front to steady himself. The landscape has smoothed, crossing low, billowing hills where cattle graze. His awe at the vastness of this country has never left him, and he suspects never will. It's a far cry from the noisy, constricted alleys of the East End of London where he grew up.

They reach the bus station in a sunlit Cooma by lunchtime. Alf goes to the counter where an older man dressed in company uniform asks him his destination.

'Melbourne.' Alf glances at the timetable pasted to the wall. 'Are there seats left on this afternoon's?'

The man examines a sheet of paper on the counter. 'Plenty. Want one?'

Alf hesitates, and declines. It's a moment of optimism, in case the Libby miracle happens. He leaves his suitcase at the bus station in any case, and doesn't book into a hotel, instead wandering Sharpe Street to mingle with the shoppers and eat a quick sandwich before presenting himself at Libby's flat. He could go to the hospital, see if she's at work. He could. And if he does, he might run into

June. He turns his back on the hospital.

◇◇◇◇◇

The sheets on the line hang languorously, soaking up warmish sunlight. Which is what June is doing, lying on a rug in the too-long grass dotted with dandelions. She's reading the library's copy of *The Go-Between* and wondering at the selfishness of lovesick adults to involve a susceptible boy in their furtive affairs. The book has, as desired, taken herself out of her own affairs, despite its irritating plot. She is restless, ill-at-ease beneath the façade of her relaxed body.

While she's working, she's able to close her mind to Peter's assumptions. When she's at home and has time to think, they churn her stomach. She goes over the mantra: she likes Peter, he's kind and thoughtful, he loves her, and she could do many times worse. The mantra doesn't squash her sense of being in a relationship with a flooded stream, with its helpless momentum and fear of being drowned in an unrelenting torrent. She turns back a page, having no idea what's going on with Leo, Ted and Marian, gives up, sets the open book on the rug and rests her head on her folded arms. Children shout in play in a neighbour's garden. A bee buzzes close by, drifts away. The scent of grass fills her nostrils. She wants to doze, let her churning stomach settle. She can't. Her mind buzzes like the bee.

When the telephone rings, June ignores it. It will be for the hairdresser, who shortly appears on the verandah, waving and calling June's name.

'Phone for you. Have to rush, in the middle of a perm.' She flees down the wide hall.

June breathes deeply, pushes herself up, taking her time. It will be Peter, telling her what time he'll collect her this evening, where they are going, what she should wear, what she'll have for dinner. She picks up the receiver, holds it briefly as she considers setting it in its cradle and later pretending she was out. Childish games.

'Hello, June here.'

'You're not gonna believe this. She's bloody well turned up.'

Peter's strident voice bellows down the line. June moves the phone from her ear.

She? Turned up?

'Leah? Do you mean Leah has come home?' Her first reaction is relief. If Leah is home, June has time to sort herself out.

'She turned up at work, wandered in, head up. Looked scared.' His voice softens and he pauses.

Poor Leah. June would be scared too. She waits on the phone, surprised at how disengaged she is from this news, as if she's listening to a wireless play and not real life.

'She told me what happened to her, let it all come out, and now she wants to come home. Be a mother to the kids, a wife to me, is what she says.' He growls. 'Said my letter gave her the courage she needed, said it made her think me and the kids would forgive her.'

'Uh huh.' The letter meant to solve all the problems. June clamps down an unexpected, nervous giggle.

'Like it's easy, just like that, after nearly two years without a word.'

June's interest is piqued. 'What did happen?'

'Nervous breakdown, she says. Depression and living off medication the damn doctor prescribed and which made things worse. Never told me about it. Ended up terrified she might hurt herself or, God forbid, the kids. Felt she had to leave us and find help somewhere else.'

All this went on and Peter had no idea? June remembers him telling her how Leah could be moody, 'like all women'. His wife had been suffering and unable to tell him. It's not hard to imagine it. June has seen enough women – and men – unable to seek or find help, who end up in hospital beds with bandaged wrists or pumped stomachs.

'Will you take her back?' She makes her voice neutral,

not sure what she wants him to say.

Peter splutters in her ear. 'Of course not. How can I? I have you, June, you're the woman I want. I'll tell her I still want a divorce, and quickly.'

As June understands the legal process, there is no 'quickly' given events have turned this way. She stares along the dim hallway to the sunshine outside.

Leah has come home. Contrite. Not a woman who deserted her family for the high life in the Big Smoke. More a heroine. June imagines Leah's suffering, her inability to confide in the one person who should have been there to help her, the agony of the choices she was compelled to make. And the courage it took for her to return to her unknowing husband.

And finally, with the abruptness of stepping off a cliff edge, everything falls into place. The kaleidoscope of emotions and desires, of what June really wants, arrange themselves into sharp-edged clarity.

'Peter.'

'Yes?'

'Leah is your wife and your children's mother. You're being given a second chance to bring your family together, to make things right. Take it.'

'Take it?' He splutters. 'What about us? What about our plans?'

'Your plans, if I'm honest, not mine.' She sighs heavily to make sure he hears it at the other end of the line. 'You're a good man, Peter, but we wouldn't have been happy together.'

'We are happy!' His protests are too much. 'I would make you happy. It's what I want to do, look after you, care for you, give you a wonderful life.'

'It's what you believe, yes. Have you ever thought to ask what I want?' She draws a breath and plunges in. 'I suspect you never asked Leah either, beyond what colour the walls should be painted or choice of carpet. Think about it, Peter.

Look at things from her side. It might surprise you.'

'I've no idea what you're talking about. I gave her everything, and look how she repaid me!' He's shouting.

'I can't tell you about Leah, I wasn't there.' June keeps her tone mild. 'I can only talk about myself.'

Silence for a beat, two. 'Are you breaking up with me, June?' His reproachful tone tells her he hasn't taken in a word. He might later.

'Yes. Can't you see? You have responsibilities, and whether or not you and Leah can work it out, successfully or not, I can't and won't be any part of that. It's unfair on everybody, including Ben and Debbie.' A low thrust, though true.

'It won't work out. It can't.' He's sullen. 'You and I had our future planned. She can't waltz in when she feels like it and destroy it all. You'll wait for me, June, I know you will.'

'No, I won't.' She can be kind now. The worst is over. 'I'll always think of you with fondness and, however things turn out, I wish you true happiness.'

'True happiness?' His sarcasm is thick. 'Well, thank *you*, Miss Lovell.'

She thrusts the receiver away, flinching at the thump that tells her he's hung up, furious at being thwarted.

June is more careful, placing the receiver in its cradle with the same tenderness she would handle a newborn babe. She stands, staring into the garden. Her pulse beats hard at the audacity of what she has done. At the same time, she's lightheaded with relief. The swollen river had spun her in circles, dizzying her into an inability to think. Leah tossed her a life-saving rope, and June clung to it to haul herself from the eddying waters.

She laughs out loud at the melodramatic image. Her other neighbour comes out of her door, washing basket in her arms. She glances at June giggling by the telephone.

'Good news?'

'Yes and no.' June ushers the woman to go out first,

follows her, collects *The Go-Between* and her rug and returns to her flat.

She's pouring water into the kettle, her gut still fluttering, when she's overcome with deep regret for a lost chance.

The regret is not for Peter. What she's seeing is the wistfulness in Alf's eyes. She's certain it was for her.

◇◇◇◇◇

Libby is at home, in her dressing gown, the smell of toast pervading her two-room flat when Alf arrives.

'Alf! What the hell?' Libby hugs the dressing gown around herself, giggles.

He's embarrassed at having caught her like this. He should have been more considerate.

'Getting up or going to bed?' It's what pops into his head, and it's not glittering stars and cooing doves.

His embarrassment isn't shared. Libby pulls the door wider, invites him in and waves him to the sofa. 'Brilliant timing, just getting up. Didn't expect you for a few days yet, so this is a lovely surprise.'

'Thanks.' Alf pauses. He's expected to say he couldn't wait any longer, he was dying to see her. Only, like she doesn't share his embarrassment, he can't share her delight at his unexpected appearance.

God, this is hard. He swallows, plays it straight.

'It's kind of hello, and goodbye, in a way.'

Libby's eyebrows arch, her smile rounds itself into an Oh.

Alf plunges on. 'Had enough of tunnels and mountains. I'm going home.'

'Ah.' Her face is blank.

He owes her more than this. 'It's a beautiful day. Can we go for a walk and I can explain? There's a place I remember, right here in town, with a great view – what's it called?'

'Nanny Goat Hill.'

'That's it. And coffee at the Italian place afterwards?'

'Sure.'

Her voice is neutral, as if she's waiting to see how this will play out. Alf hopes he can be gracious, kind, and not hurt this bubbly, fun girl. He hopes he's laid sufficient groundwork in his factual, friendly and unromantic letters. He hopes he hasn't underestimated Libby's feelings and fantasies.

'Let me get dressed, huh?' Her giggle this time might be a release of tension. Or she thinks Alf is playing a joke. 'Don't think Cooma is ready for me in my PJs in the middle of the day.' She waves to the sofa again. 'Take a pew. Won't be long.'

Twenty minutes later, they're climbing the path to the lookout. Their lack of chat, bar Alf's comment about recognising the way, is partially disguised by the chettering of galahs flocking in a flurry of pink and white feathers in the surrounding stunted eucalypts.

Libby doesn't ask about his earlier visit to the lookout, how he found the place, who he was with. Alf's glad. Is he deliberately re-enacting a scene from three years ago? An exorcism? Expunge memories and the emotions which come with them?

Libby stands before the tall stone outcrop and opens her arms to the view. 'I love this place.'

Alf can see why. The township spreads below, its white corrugated iron roofs pristine in the afternoon sunlight, broken up by the occasional red roof. A smattering of older stone buildings with steep gables trimmed in white peer down their aristocratic noses at their humble, square neighbours. Beyond the town are the brown plains he crossed in the bus from Jindabyne this morning, and beyond them, ancient tree-covered mountains innocent of the busy work going on to reshape their innards.

Alf takes it all in. A short climb and here is distance, clarity. His way forward is clear, although it brings him no peace.

Libby thrusts her hands in her trouser pockets, stares

out over the rooftops. 'Going home.'

She makes it sound a defeat. Alf supposes it is, given he's achieved nothing by coming here except a healthier savings balance.

'Yes.' He's trying to add a reason beyond, *I didn't like it up there*, when Libby swivels to face him. Her eyes are sad and Alf is a monster for making them so.

'There never was going to be anything beyond good friends between us, was there?' She gently presses her palm to his chest, as if testing whether blood pumps through his body.

'Libby, I –'

'It's okay.' She purses her lips, shrugs. 'I'm a grown girl. And old and wise enough to understand when a man's feelings aren't what I'd like them to be.'

'You don't want to be bogged down with me, Libby.' Alf holds her gaze. 'I'm dull, boring. You're the kind of woman who needs liveliness, activity, adventure.'

'And where am I to find liveliness, activity and adventure here, unless it's with a brooding, good-looking stranger?' The veneer of humour lies thinly over her bitterness.

Brooding? Good-looking? Him? She's thinking of Teddy, has the two of them mixed up. He pushes the thought away, along with the implication of Libby's question.

'Why don't you leave here, go to Sydney or Melbourne? More life there.'

'I should. It's definitely crossed my mind before.' She turns aside but Alf spots the quick bite of her top lip. 'Maybe this is the time to take my shattered heart there.'

'I'm sorry, I truly am.' He is sorry, but he can't lie, pretend something exists when it never did.

Libby turns back to him, squints. 'Is it Raine?' She digs her hands deeper into her pockets, her tone accusing. 'Don't you think you've carried a torch for her long enough? How many years?'

'Raine?' How does Libby…? June, of course. Alf's

automatic response is denial. 'No.' Yet as he says it, he understands his denial is accurate. He thinks of Raine's letter, of his reluctance to rush home, of his conviction she and Teddy have to sort their own messes. It honestly isn't about Raine.

'Tut.' Libby scowls. 'I think it is, and you need to get over it, if not for me, then for anyone else you meet.'

Alf shakes his head. 'To be honest, part of why I came up here was to rid myself of that particular ghost.'

He waves towards the mountains. Stubborn patches of snow lie scattered on the heights, and in his current contemplative mood Alf likens them to the remnants of his love for Raine.

'I think it worked. Being in those mountains, facing up to the challenges they throw in your face every day … does a lot to clear your thinking.'

Libby tilts her head to the side. 'I believe you.'

She doesn't sound as if she believes him, which is all right because Alf believes himself. He waits to feel lighter for the admission. Nothing. The weight in his gut doesn't dissolve.

Libby wraps her arms about herself and squeezes tight against a growing coolness. A wind has risen, trailing the cold of those snowy patches. The shadow of the piled rocks behind them lengthens, casts out the warming sun. Alf is chilled too. He struggles to find a kind, encouraging, parting word, and fails.

'There's somebody though, whether you know it or not.' Libby's accusation is sharp. She keeps her face to the view, adopts a conciliatory tone. 'I hope you find that person, Alf, and I wish you all happiness when you do.'

'And you. There's a lucky bloke out there for you, I'm certain there is.' He sounds trite.

Libby throws out her hands, questioning his assumption. 'Have a good journey home.' She stalks off down the track to town, swinging her arms in time with her long strides.

Walking in the Rain

Alf waits, his brain picking at the conversation. He's over Raine. Yes. There's someone else. Yes. And that someone else is as unavailable to him as Raine has always been. He shivers, walks the circumference of the lookout, not seeing what's out there, his mind fixed on his own hopelessness.

In less than an hour, he'll be on the bus to Melbourne, heading home. He'll have plenty of time to think about what he's learned, gained – lost – from his mountain experience. It will have to do.

Chapter Thirteen

AFTER HER CALL WITH PETER, June takes comfort on the sofa. As the afternoon grows darker and chillier, she wraps herself in a blanket, listens to the wireless and tries to make sense of everything her babbling emotions throw at her.

Her relief, the lightness at not having to pretend she loves Peter or wants to be with him forever, brings a second, giddying freedom. The freedom to confess she loves Alf, that her tentative steps down that path three years ago were merely halted, not withdrawn, by his inability to respond.

It's her one certainty. Going over their few interactions the week he was here, she lets herself examine them in a new light: that Alf possibly loves her. The fact of his return to Cooma where he must have realised he would come back into her life; the shared glance at the dinner; the searing soul-searching on the path outside Peter's office.

June believes, is almost one hundred percent sure, her relationship with Peter stifled any words Alf might want to say to her. What brilliant timing, being with someone exactly at the wrong moment.

Alf didn't look you up when he first arrived, a nasty voice insinuates. True, and it hurt. She draws up excuses. Alf is quiet, withdrawn. He might have gotten cold feet, or was gathering his courage, and when he saw her at the hospital she was unfriendly. By then he'd met Peter and learned of her so-called engagement. And now there is Libby to think of, with her happiness in Alf's careful hands. A comedy of errors. Someone should write a play about it. Ha.

She's restless, should eat. The idea of food holds no appeal. Deciding a soak in the bath is what she needs, she undresses and with her dressing gown loose about her, lights the chip heater with a whump of gas. She's running the taps when there's a knock at her door. Damn. It's likely Peter, coming in person to tell her he'll not take no for an answer. She'll ignore it.

'June!' Rap rap. 'June, it's me, Libby. Are you there?'

There's a creak as the flat door opens – June must make sure she locks it when she's here – and Libby's loud voice demands entry.

June sighs. 'In here, hold on.' She turns off the taps and the heater, and goes to greet her guest.

Libby puts her hand to her mouth, sways from side to side. Her eyelids are swollen, mascara streaking her cheeks.

'Libby! What's happened?'

'Can we talk? Please. There's no one else I can unload to, and if I don't get this out of my system, I'll burst.'

Drama in Libby's life isn't new. To be this worked up about it is.

'Cup of tea? Something stronger? There's a beer in the ice chest.'

'Tea, tea is fine.' Libby plumps onto the sofa, still wearing her coat, and puts her head in her hands.

June leaves her there to fill the kettle and put it on to boil.

Libby doesn't wait for tea. She launches straight in. 'What's wrong with me, June?' She raises her head, and June is distressed to see tears running down her friend's face.

'What's wrong with you? Nothing!' June is confused. A day ago, Libby was on top form, crowing about Alf visiting and what a great time they'd have and … Alf? Is this to do with Alf?

She leaves the kettle and sits beside Libby, an arm around her shoulder.

'Tell me.'

'Alf came.' Sniff. 'Earlier than I thought, today.' Libby draws a hankie from her coat pocket and wipes her nose.

'You didn't expect him until next week, right?'

Libby nods.

'What happened?' June assumes there's no good news of blossoming romance, of Alf whisking Libby home to show her off to his friends, introducing her to Raine and

Teddy and the kids. She holds her breath, waiting.

'He broke up with me. Tells me there's no future for us.' Her voice is quiet, girlish, hurt.

'Broke up?' June's traitorous heart lurches. She rebukes it. Her role here is as comforter.

'Yes, broke up. Half an hour ago. He came by after lunch, I was barely awake after my shift, and he turns up and of course I was thrilled to see him.' Libby scrubs at her eyes with the damp hankie. June should fetch a clean one. In a moment.

'He wanted to go to the lookout, to *explain*. Ha!'

'Nanny Goat Hill?'

'Yes.'

A tremor runs through June, reliving what happened the day she took Alf there. Did he tell Libby he'd been there with her?

'And out it all came. No future for us.' She grabs June's hand. 'You remember how we talked about him still carrying a torch for Raine?'

'Yes.' Is it true? After all this time? The tremor jolts to a stop.

'I asked him.' Libby grimaces. 'Well, accused him, of still wanting her and how he'd never love anyone if he kept on with his useless dreams.'

June winces. 'Ah. Did he confess?'

'He said no, it was why he'd come to the mountains, to lay that ghost to rest, to use his own words.' Libby wriggles about to face June, her eyes puffy and her face pale. 'My guess is there's someone else, there's someone Alf loves. And I'm betting that someone is as off limits as Raine.' She whooshes out a breath. 'Almost makes me feel sorry for the bugger.'

'Poor Libby.' June tightens her hold on her friend's shoulders while her mind leapfrogs from one hopeful not-to-be-said-out-loud thought to another. 'Maybe Alf needs time, to sort himself out.'

'He can have all the time he wants.' Libby's tartness indicates the beginning of her road to recovery. 'His endless trip home will be a good start.'

'Home?' June didn't mean it to come out this sharply.

'Yep. For all I know he took this afternoon's bus. Probably had the ticket in his pocket all the time he was telling me the bad news.' She snorts, angry. 'Callous bastard. No hanging about.'

A cry struggles up June's throat. She clamps it down. 'Oh.'

When Libby has had her tea and comfort, dried her eyes and mocked herself about going back to kissing frogs, June waves her goodbye, makes herself a cheese toastie, fresh tea, and sits on the sofa. She eats the food, not tasting it. She realises she didn't tell Libby about Leah and her own 'breaking up' phone call with Peter. It can wait. Alf is more on her mind than Peter.

Alf chose Nanny Goat Hill as the place to tell Libby it wasn't going to work between them. And they were at the lookout right at the time June was telling Peter it wasn't going to work for them. Fate.

Except now, Alf is on his way home, and June's chance to look in his eyes and test the truth of what she hopes, believes … that chance is on a bus miles away.

Or is it? Libby wasn't certain about the bus. In a sudden rush of energy, June launches off the sofa and lurches into the hallway. The bus station number is on a pad on the wall, alongside those of the railway station, taxi company, the hospital and nearest GP. She dials the bus number.

'I was wondering if you could tell me if a friend of mine managed to catch the bus to Melbourne this afternoon. He was running late, and I was worried he wouldn't make it.'

'Name?' The man's voice is bored, uncaring of June's lie. Doubtless he's heard them all before.

'Alf Hall.'

'Hmm … yeah, he's there. Bought a ticket in the nick of

time.'

'Oh, good, good, thank you.'

'Any time.' He hangs up.

June stays in the hall, rubbing her chin. In the nick of time? Libby is wrong. Alf isn't a callous bastard after all.

◇◇◇◇◇

Sleep comes in pieces, none of them refreshing. Alf sits on the aisle, two rows from the front on the non-driver side. The road ahead is swept by the wide, flat-fronted coach's dual headlights. Trees rush from shadowed darkness like an attacking army, to be swept aside as the driver steers smoothly around bends, some tighter than others. Alf's previous journeys on this road have been in daylight, and he conjures images of the hilly, tree-strewn landscape, offset by occasional cleared areas where farms have dug in, their post and wire fences barricading any attempted repossession by the displaced bush.

They make stops in sleeping townships where passengers are collected by men driving utes. The hills soften as the road continues south. The landscape emerges from the dark in a series of lightening shades of grey which turn to green under the sun's alchemy.

In between snatches of sleep, Alf's brain jumps from Libby's sad eyes and squinting accusations to her long-legged stride down the track from Nanny Goat Hill. He's sorry to have caused her pain, comforts himself it was needed to avoid greater pain later.

Other, more insistent, images leap about in his head. They are of June, of the soul-searching look that passed between them outside Peter's office before he went to the camp, and of her last words to him: 'Make the most of the mountains, Alf. Work it out.' He's more and more sure of the softly added, 'Please', which he may or may not have been meant to hear.

The townships they pass grow into towns. They pause for a breakfast break and once more for an early lunch. The road widens, thickens with traffic, and the trees lining the streets of Melbourne's eastern suburbs gaze graciously on the coach, which slows in response. They reach the terminal at the bottom end of the city by mid-afternoon. Alf's eyes are gritty, his clothes grimy, so after he's bought his fancy sleeper ticket for the overnight train home, he searches out a cheap hotel room near the railway station. He can shower there and leave his suitcase for a few hours.

Cleaner and wide awake, he wanders past the tall elegance of the Savoy Plaza, hesitates, and decides on less expensive food from the nearby Victoria market. Exploring the stalls with their increasingly exotic, European produce diverts him until it's time to collect his case and settle on the train. At last exhausted by his travel, he sleeps, with shallow awakenings at the infrequent stops with their lit platforms and piercing guards' whistles. At the end of the line, he steps off the train and walks with his bleary-eyed fellow passengers along the wide tarmac of the inner halls, past the cafés, key cutters and shoe repairers, and up into a pearly dawn.

He is back where he started, three months ago.

◇◇◇◇◇

The day creeps along. June's mind tracks Alf's journey, as it did for much of the night. She measures her hours in terms of where he might be at any one time – out of New South Wales and well into Victoria, travelling the coast road, past the coal towns with their self-made black clouds and across lush dairy country. She knows the arrival time in Melbourne and is curious as to whether Alf will travel the last leg home by bus or train, and will he do another overnighter or take a break?

Why is she punishing herself? He's gone. With no farewell. June mulls this over. Does it mean Alf couldn't care less about her, not even as a friend? Or – she summons the wistful look on the gravel path outside Peter's office – he didn't dare risk seeing her because she belongs with

Peter? Belonged with Peter, past tense.

She's in the small, windowless pharmacy measuring medications for the patients' evening dosages when Stella pokes her head around the door.

'Ah, there you are. Was about to give up and say I couldn't find you.'

'Give up on what?'

'There's someone in reception keen to see you.'

'Oh?' June's heart thumps. 'It's not Peter, is it?' She hears the cowardice in her voice.

Stella arches her brows. 'No, I'd have said if it was him. A woman, didn't give her name.' She frowns. 'Has something happened between you and Mr Perfect?'

'Can you take over doing this?' June points to a line on the list. 'I've done Mr Parker's, there's only a few to go.'

'Sure.' Stella moves to swap places with June. 'As long as you promise to tell all once you've done with visiting.' She shoos her out the door. 'Off you go.'

June walks along the corridors and turns into the foyer. A woman stands staring out the window, across the wide verandah to the street. She's wearing a trench coat, and a plain dark tan hat perches at an angle on her head.

June coughs. 'Hello? Are you looking for me?'

The woman starts, pivots about. Her open coat reveals a straight tweed skirt and a buttoned dark green cardigan. A brown scarf hangs loosely about her neck. The plainness of her clothing complements her faded blonde prettiness, her one concession to strong colour being a dab of red lipstick.

'June?' The woman's pale blue eyes twitch, as if she is nervous.

'Yes.'

'We've never met. I'm Leah Adams, Peter's wife.'

June jerks back. 'Ah.'

June's imagined Leah, when she thought of her at all, was built from her scraps of conversation with Libby and from Peter's hesitant talk of his wife. In her mind, Leah was colourful, sophisticated, with her airs about being from the capital and her choice of modern Danish furniture.

She might have been, before. Today she's the essence of frowsy, suburban motherhood. June wonders where and when the transformation happened, if there's been a transformation.

Leah presses her red lips together. 'Yes, the lost sheep wife.' She swallows. 'Peter told me about you, about you and him.'

June draws in a breath, exhales. 'Not a lot to tell.' She is wary. Has Leah come to accuse her of … of what?

'Not a lot to tell. That's what he said.' Leah takes a step closer to peer intently into June's face. Her eyes are sad. 'I wanted to check for myself.' She wrings her hands. 'I acted badly, very badly, and I've no right to turn up out of the blue and expect Peter to take me in.'

'You were ill.' June's caring instincts kick in, all tea and sympathy after this confession.

'Yes, and I should have talked to Peter earlier and asked for his help, only … well … I didn't.'

June understands. Peter has no ability to take in anything which might splinter his perfect world. A troubled wife would have been as uncomfortable as looking into one of those distorted fairground mirrors, without the mirth.

Leah plunges on. 'And if he's found someone else, I'd be in the wrong all over again to stand in his way.' Her lips quiver, her eyes are moist.

June's eyes well too. This woman has been through a terrible, terrible time, and she's blaming herself for all of it. And, to top it off, proposing martyrdom to allow the man who drove her to this – or at best was insufficiently attentive to spot there was a problem – to have his happy ever after.

Anger, not at Leah, rudely brushes through June's sympathy, elbows bent. She gabbles, wanting to get this out, to be clear, and be done with it for all time.

'Listen, Leah, believe me when I say there's no me and him.' She pauses a second at the widening of Leah's eyes. 'Frankly, there never was on my part, and I was stupid for letting Peter think so, especially once I knew he wasn't divorced.' She takes a quick intake of air and hurries on. 'I'm thrilled you've come home, mostly for the kids' sake. They must be over the moon to have their mummy after all this time, and I honestly, with all sincerity, hope you and Peter work through it and can be a family again.'

Leah stares at her. 'You don't mind I'm back?'

'No.' June is emphatic, and means it. 'From what Peter told me, you acted the best way you could given you were sick, and suffering. And after all you've been through, you deserve to have your family around you.' She huffs. 'Hopefully Peter will take better care of you this time.'

'Take better care?' Leah's eyelids flicker, taking in this different view of events. 'I'm glad you understand.'

June opens her mouth to offer further reassurance, except Leah carries on.

'Do you think you and I could be friends?' She flushes pale pink. 'The children appear to like you a lot. They'll miss you, I think.'

Friends? What planet is this woman on? The one where she has no clue what her husband is like, sadly. Not June's business.

'Umm, yes, of course.' She brightens her tone. 'I'm going away though, so it'll have to wait. Meanwhile, you have my sincerest best wishes for the future.' She glances behind her, towards the wards. 'And I don't mean to be rude, but I have to see to my patients.'

'Oh yes, of course, I'm sorry.' Leah offers June her hand and a tentative smile. 'Thank you. I was terrified of coming to see you, and I'm glad, thrilled, you're okay about it all. Thank you.'

June takes the cool, dry hand, shakes it briefly, says

goodbye and stays long enough to see Leah walk out into the evening. Poor woman.

As she hurries to the pharmacy, June thinks over the conversation. Peter told his wife there was little to tell about him and June. No threats of continuing with the divorce. June is comforted. Her suspicions Peter hadn't stopped loving his wife, or at least wanted her home, are vindicated. His perfect world can be restored without messy divorces and the gossip which comes with it. There will still be gossip, of course, about the prodigal wife, but Peter will be seen as gracious, forgiving and able to fulfil his role as protector and provider to a woman who is grateful.

Handing out medications, June moves from the conversation with Leah to hearing her own words, about going away. Unthought of until the moment she said them, remembered only now. She gasps softly.

Yes, of course.

Didn't June once tell Libby Alf might need a push? Or a great bloody shove. There's one way to find out the truth. She laughs out loud and receives a guilty glance from old Mrs Nelson, trying to hide her pills under her pillow.

Chapter Fourteen

With no home of his own to go to and his bike under wraps in Teddy's crumbling garden shed, Alf heads there, catching the tram in the opposite direction to the crowd of commuters travelling into the city.

Raine is expecting him, courtesy of Alf's telegram from Melbourne. He winced after he sent it, remembering too late Teddy's fateful telegram from the same post office three years ago, and the grief it caused. Raine hasn't appeared to notice the blunder. She welcomes him with a hug and a teasing laugh.

'Couldn't stay away, hey?'

When the kids have said hi as if Alf had visited yesterday, and are settled with toys in the big lounge, Raine makes tea. She and Alf sit at the kitchen table cradling warm mugs, again as if it was yesterday. Alf is sinking into his old, unthinking life. It's like shrugging into a comfortable, shabby coat. Something has changed though.

He gestures at the dining room. 'Teddy's started work at last.'

The peeling wallpaper is stripped, highlighting a plaster patchwork from different decades and in varying conditions. Blotches of shades of green paint show someone has been testing colours.

Raine nods. 'The lounge room's next. Teddy's been working on the heavy stuff in the evenings, now it's lighter and warmer. I pitch in on the weekends if the kids let me.' She raises her mug to Alf. 'Here's to house progress!'

'And Teddy's business?' Alf raises his eyebrows. 'After your letter, I was expecting the worst.'

Raine sips her tea. 'Me too.' She whooshes out a breath. 'We had a real set-to over it. It was Mr Greene, bless him, brought Teddy to his senses.'

'Oh? What miracle did he perform?'

Raine smirks. 'I asked him, and he said he sat his son

down and gave him a hard talking to about the realities of running a business and his responsibilities as a husband and father.'

'Teddy listened?'

'Yes. Came home full of being sorry, saying he hadn't taken in how bad things were, and he'll listen when me and his dad say he's spending too much time on pieces. But –' Raine throws out her arms '– he'll be the one to decide when a chair, a cabinet, a table is ready to go to the customer.'

Alf tilts his chair back. 'It's a start, I guess.' He brings the chair forward with a thump. 'Is it enough, do you think?'

'Could be a breakthrough, given I have a powerful ally to bolster me.' She crosses her arms on the table and winks. 'With you here, two allies.'

'Hmm. I'll try.' For what it would be worth, as ever.

Raine gets up to refill the teapot. 'Here we are rabbiting on about Teddy, and you haven't told me what happened in Cooma. Your letters weren't exactly gossipy.' She sets the kettle on the stove. 'Did you see Nurse June?' Her tone is deliberate, casual.

Alf's letters have been big on superficial facts and low on interpretation. Libby was absent all together – a clue to his true feelings for her. He hopes she's all right, or getting there fast.

'Hello, off with the fairies there, Alf.' Raine pours more tea into his mug and peers at him, quizzical. 'Either a lot happened, or nothing. Which is it? C'mon, 'fess up.'

A lot or nothing? Alf considers the question. Neither description suits. It wasn't a lot. Neither was it nothing. Not for him, not for Libby. As for June –

'Nurse June is engaged.' He takes a deliberate swig of tea, hoping to hide any emotion his eyes might show.

'Oh.' Raine squints at him, her eyes questioning.

'Makes nonsense of all Arthur's stupid teasing.' Alf's attempt at humour comes out more of a snort. His neck warms. 'Arthur wouldn't have known, of course.'

'I'm pleased for her.' Raine drums her fingers on the table. 'Did you meet him? Is he a good man?'

'I worked for him, briefly, in Cooma.' Alf lets the second question fade away. He has no wish to talk about Peter. Or June. He takes his mug to the sink and rinses it. 'Going to take the bike out for a spin, make sure it works.'

'Good idea.' Raine frowns towards the hall. 'Far too quiet, better go check on them.'

Alf collects his suitcase and carries it to the spare room. When he's dressed in his leathers, he puts his head around the lounge door where Raine and the kids are lying on the floor putting together a wooden jigsaw puzzle with oversized pieces.

'I'll see you later.' He waves and goes outside to free his bike from its cover and chain.

◇◇◇◇◇

The familiarity of the road winding up through the hills to Teddy and Raine's old cabin does nothing to soothe Alf's restlessness. It's more of the same old, same old, and he's deliberately sinking himself into it, given he has no reason to ride here except nostalgia. If nostalgia is the right word, with its implications of more contented times. In the days when Teddy was missing, when Alf was being a 'terrific friend' to Raine, and she took his friendship at face value and loved him for it … Alf thought himself content at least. A fool's paradise.

He turns off the road at the farm track and rides slowly, waveringly, up its rutted, stony slope under the quiet gaze of the eucalypts. When he reaches the cabin, he switches off the bike's engine and stretches his legs to balance himself.

The cabin's split log walls and narrow verandah hunker under the shelter of the red gum. No smoke curls from the chimney. No curtains hang at the windows. Raine's precious vegetable patch has gone to seed, and Teddy's woodshed with its extravagant hammerbeam roof could do with a fresh coat of stain.

Walking in the Rain

Alf waits for the kookaburra's mocking call. Nothing. The day's brightness has dulled. The blue sky is locked behind a wall of roiling cloud, shushing the magpies' warbling and the chet chet nattering of strident galahs. The silent greyness suits his melancholy mood.

Old emotions swirl. Alf shrugs them off with an annoyed snort. He's done with them. He didn't lie to Libby when he said he was over Raine. Something new has taken their place. Libby was right when she accused him of loving another woman. And yet again, his love is mistimed, misplaced. He sits astride his bike, stares at the forlorn cabin. He should move in, two lost souls together. Alf is not given to self-pity. It's anger which stirs in his chest, anger with himself.

Heavy drops of rain fall, sparse, and loud as a doomsday drumming on the cabin's corrugated roof. Alf squints into the leaden sky as the drops gather momentum. Bloody weather.

He doesn't bother with taking a peek inside to see if the stains on the ceiling have spread, or to walk around to check the windows are intact. He turns the bike, kick starts it into life and roars off through the rain with no glance back. The present occupies his head, not the past, and in the present he is disconsolate, unhappy with the world.

He skids the bike to a halt at the bottom of the track, revs the engine, barely glances left and right and accelerates into the wetness and onto the road. He opens the throttle and hares around the bends, hardly slowing at the switchback.

The bike slides on the shiny wetness, tips towards the asphalt. A terrifying moment of falling, uncontrolled. Alf hauls hard, struggles, gets himself and the bike upright. He slows to a juddering stop by the opposite bank, away from the drop into the treed valley.

Breathing hard, shaking, Alf stares behind him at the grooves in the wet gravel. He slips off the bike and manages to kick the stand into place before sinking to the ground, where he draws his knees to his chin. He squeezes his eyes tight shut, blocking the image of him and the bike falling through rain and trees, his shredded body pinned under the hot engine, the motor roaring, wheels spinning.

A long, grey car stops, a window is rolled down, and a middle-aged man in a brown hat peers at Alf through the sheeting rain. Leaning across from the passenger seat, a woman stares with anxious eyes.

'You okay, mate?' The man rests his elbow on the door's window frame. 'Saw you nearly lose it, thought you were over the edge and dead for sure.'

'Thanks.' With an effort, Alf stands, stiffening his trembling legs. 'Yeah. Thought I was dead too.'

'Need a lift anywhere?'

'Nah, thanks all the same.' Alf grabs the motorcycle's handles. 'I'll take it easy the rest of the way.'

'Yeah, good idea.'

The man waits while Alf turns the key, lets the engine idle for a moment and moves slowly off. The car passes him, the man giving a tight wave through the closed window. The car's red rear lights travel steadily away from Alf, swallowed by the weather and the next curve hugging the hillside.

The rain decides it's given Alf a hard enough time. The deluge quietens, the clouds break apart and a cheery sun sends long fingers of white light to polish the puddles to a dazzling glow.

Alf's confidence returns with the sunshine. His stomach settles, his brain stops its looping somersaults.

As dazzlingly clear as the sun, he understands what he has to do.

Chapter Fifteen

JUNE'S EXHILARATION LASTS THE LENGTH of the telephone call to the bus station to book a ticket to Melbourne for the next morning – done from the hospital before she can change her mind – and through packing a few clothes. The elation of purposeful action also carries her through a late meal of scrambled eggs. In bed, however, June's tired body fails to convince her brain it needs rest. Doubts buzz in her skull like bushflies around a dead sheep, and as toxic.

She lies staring at the moon-washed ceiling. What idiocy is she about to commit? Not necessarily idiocy. Rational thought squeezes its thin presence into her head, to swipe at the doubts. It insists there is another, valid, reason for this journey, the one June told Leah. A short holiday, well-deserved.

Holding this pretence firmly to her fluttering chest, June sleeps, wakes, sleeps, and wakes to the alarm. A quick cup of tea, a wash, latching her brown suitcase, and she's out the door into a cool, dark dawn without allowing herself thinking time.

But the bus is barely out of Cooma when her desire to scream, 'Stop!', run down the narrow aisle and fall out onto the road, is strong enough to force her to clamp her mouth shut.

It's more than the possibility of rejection. To be rejected, she first has to find Alf. With no address, finding an A Hall in the telephone directory, assuming he has a phone, could be a long task. Before setting out, she had the sense to look up the hospital records to remind herself of Raine and Teddy's surname. She knows they now live by the beach, which narrows it a little. She hopes to God they have a phone. It's a tenuous hope. She clenches her fists in her lap and stares straight ahead.

And if she does find Alf? Who left with no goodbye, even as a friend. Whose actions over three years say he has little feeling for her. But his eyes ... they tell a different tale.

No, it's reckless, ill-advised. A stupid idea altogether.

She'll leave the bus at the first stop and turn right around.

'Nervous traveller?' The woman on the aisle turns to June. 'Don't blame you, the way some of these drivers take the bends.' She pats June's arm. 'This one's careful, you don't need to worry.'

June murmurs an assurance about being fine, thank you.

'Good, good.' The woman smiles through freshly coloured, bright red lips. 'Holiday or business?'

'Umm, holiday.' Yes, holiday.

When June fails to return the question, the woman pulls a *Women's Weekly* magazine from her over-large handbag and settles it on her knees.

June leans back in her seat with a soft sigh and turns her head to stare at the paddocks where tractors plough the spring soil, or sheep and cattle graze the new green grasses. In the rare townships, cars and utes – dogs pacing the open trays – park at an angle to concrete kerbs while their owners walk in and out of shops displaying goods crowded behind plate glass. Alf passed through here two nights ago, seeing only blackness and a rare light from a distant house.

Through it all, June battles the devils of doubt. It's insane, making this long, uncomfortable journey on the basis of a look, a feeling, both of which sprang from her imagination, didn't they? No, they didn't. Alf wants her. It's why he came to the mountains when he could have gone anywhere in the country to escape his ghosts. Or was it that he believed Cooma, with its stark, emotional memories, was the best choice for the desired exorcism? He needed to face the ghosts head on to placate them, and having done so, he is free to return to his old life. A life June has no part in.

The bus halts at a roadside café and petrol station. Last off, June stands in a long queue with her fellow passengers waiting to use the one toilet. The cool dawn has blossomed into a perfect spring day and she lifts her face to the sun, eyes closed, grateful to be out of the bus's fuggy air.

A woman and a young girl emerge from the toilet. The girl tugs on the woman's hand. 'Will Daddy meet us at the bus station?'

'Of course. Think how much he's missed us! He's probably waiting already.' She swings the child's hand. The girl giggles.

They head into the café, the child skipping, the mother unhurried, like one who knows where she is going, why, and what – or whom – she'll find at the other end. Lucky woman.

June steps from foot to foot. She should get off here, like she promised herself, and go home. Not make a fool of herself. It's too far to go on a whim, holiday excuse or no holiday excuse.

She needs the lavatory. Then, she decides, she'll find out what time the return bus to Cooma arrives.

She'll get on with her life, just like she's done until now. She will forget Alf, as doubtless he is forgetting her. Isn't he?

◇◇◇◇◇

Alf rides to Raine and Teddy's holding his Eureka moment close, determined not to let it escape before he can act on it. At the house, he chains the bike in the shed, covers it, collects his unpacked case and searches out Raine in the kitchen peeling potatoes.

'Umm, sounds silly.' He wriggles his shoulders. 'Seems I've left something behind, have to go back.'

Raine's eyes widen. 'Left something behind? Go all that way? What on earth …?'

'I'll write and explain, promise. Don't worry.' Alf glances at the clock on the peeling wall. 'Have to go.'

She tilts her head to the side. 'Better be a long letter, with lots of explanation.' She gives him the witch look, the one where she can see inside his head, steps towards him – a potato in one hand, the paring knife in the other – and gives him a slow smile before kissing him on the cheek.

'Good luck, Alf.'

He doesn't treat himself to a sleeper this time. Too extravagant. It helps that the seat next to him is empty for the time being, and Alf stretches his legs, falls into the leather and whooshes out a loud breath. He follows it with a silent laugh.

He's mad. June is engaged to Peter. She must love him. Therefore she doesn't love Alf. Simple. He's on another fool's errand.

Except ... that kiss from three years ago, her confession she was hurt when he stopped writing to her, her belief he was still hankering for Raine ... too many misunderstandings, too much not said that should have been said.

Alf messed up right from the beginning, when he didn't go to the hospital, try and find her. No, he messed up long before then, when he let June fade from his life. Although not from his thoughts.

He has one chance left, and this time he has to say it out loud. He practises the words, mouthing them: I love you. Deep inside of me. More than you could possibly love me. I want to be with you forever.

What's the worst that can happen? June might laugh in his face. No, she's too generous to take pleasure in someone else's pain.

If she says no, no matter how kindly, Alf will return to the camps, save more money, and head off to Sydney. A proper fresh start. No more running to Teddy and Raine, to his old life and old ties. Not that he has any ties, or any that can't easily be broken.

The train heads east into a darkness scarred by a rare lit platform, an occasional cluster of town lights and the single dots of lonely homesteads perched in their wide paddocks. The clack of the wheels, the consistent swaying of the wagon, and the murmured conversations of other passengers, lull Alf's exhausted mind and body. He dozes, startles awake at the border stop where the engines are changed, accepts a mug of tea from a steward, and goes back to dozing.

In his dreams, June lifts a scornful chin at his declaration, cruelly arrogant, while Peter stalks him, fists raised, across a freezing, snowy slope where frontloaders roar, swallowing whole trees, ripping gashes from the mountain's side.

Alf wakes, sweating, mouth dry. He remains determined to see this through.

◇◇◇◇

The mattress in the cheap hotel room was hard, and for a second night June hasn't slept well. She throws off the worn chenille cover and sets her feet on the rug. Pulling on her dressing gown and grabbing her washbag, she lets herself out of her room. She's in luck. At this early hour the bathroom at the end of the hall is unoccupied. No time for a bath, but a wash, clean teeth, and brushed hair improve her sense of wellbeing. Her watch tells her she needs to move faster, and fortunately she hasn't far to go. She paid for the room in advance, so she packs her pyjamas and wash things into her case, closes it and, shrugging on her trench coat and setting her hat firmly on her head, walks along the hall and the one flight of stairs to the stark reception area.

A sleepy-eyed clerk takes her key with a grunt which might pass for a good morning greeting, and June is outside, under falling rain. She squints into the downpour and sets off quickly across the road.

There's time to change her mind. She lifts her shoulders, shifts her suitcase from her left to her right hand. No. She's made her decision. She'll stick to it.

◇◇◇◇

It's raining. Alf shouldn't be surprised, given this is a city famous for its rain and changeable weather. His watch tells him he has barely enough time to reach the bus terminal. He hopes there's a seat left.

He strides along the platform beside other disembarking passengers. An older couple struggling with their too heavy cases block his way. He reins in his impatience, waits for a gap and slides past. The queue at the barriers moves slowly, steadily forward. Alf glances again at his watch, and at last he can show his ticket and push through, his case a heavier burden than he's noticed before.

He's hurrying through the main doors, anxious he'll be too late, eyes straight ahead, concentrating. So it must be a second sense, an intuition, which makes him look twice at the woman scurrying, head bent against the rain, along the footpath towards the station entrance. She's nearly level with him, separated by jostling people and raised umbrellas. He stops, stares. The crowd grumbles and breaks either side of him.

It's her. June. On the rain-soaked footpath, about to disappear under the high stone arches to go … where?

His heart leaps. Falls. No, it couldn't be.

'June!'

With the rain and the traffic noise, they are too far apart for her to hear him. So what does it matter if she happens to be here? Likely she's come to choose a wedding dress.

It does matter. Alf's gut tells him it does. And too bad if she's here to buy a damn dress. He has to say what he has to say. He promised himself.

He pivots on his heel, pushes his way through, apologising, ignoring glares and 'Watch where you're going' mutters.

'June!'

He's behind her, close enough to reach out and touch her shoulder. Which he does.

She starts, whirls about. The momentary fear in her eyes turns first to confusion then to delight.

Delight?

They are motionless, the commuter crowd swarming around them.

Walking in the Rain

She is here, with a smile stretching her cheeks to their fullest. Her hat and trench coat are soaked. She's dropped her suitcase at her feet, and she's saying something about how she was worried she wouldn't be able to find him and, thank God and how wonderful, here he is, delivered up to her before she even had to try ...

Alf gapes, mouth open like a landed guppy. 'I was coming to you.' He manages that much, swallows. 'Shouldn't have left, not without saying ...'

She is staring at him, water dripping off her hat. Her smile is beautiful, she is beautiful. How could a woman like this ...? He shuts the thought down. Be brave, his heart urges him. He draws on all his courage, fuelled by her smiling, blue eyes. Yet still he stutters the rest.

'I ... I was ... I was coming back ... for you ...'

June's laugh is loud, joyful. And it hits him, harder than the pelting rain.

She wants him, she loves him. His heart hammers like a thousand woodpeckers have made it their home.

He drops his own case, returns June's glittering stare. The stammer retreats.

'I love you, June Lovell. Deeply love you.'

Thank you for reading *Walking in the Rain*. It was never my intention to write a sequel to *Keepers* until several readers asked for one. Mainly they were unhappy that *Keepers* left Alf loveless and alone, and they adored Alf, with his gentle ways and lost-cause love for Raine. Opinions have been divided over Raine's choice!

The challenge was to write a story which could also be read as a standalone, and I hope I've done this. And while readers now know how *Keepers* ends, I also hope it tempts people to read the first book and follow Raine, Teddy and Alf's tempestuous journey.

Please leave a review

If *Walking in the Rain* has given you an enjoyable moment of romantic escapism, I would be very grateful if you took a little time to write a review, or even just leave a rating – that's fine too. We indie authors don't have the resources of publishing houses behind us to promote our books and we rely heavily on reviews and word-of-mouth recommendations from satisfied readers to spread the word.

And be assured that I read (devour) every review!

You can leave a review on Amazon even if you haven't purchased the book from there. Go to the Amazon page for *Walking in the Rain*, where you will find the magic words 'Write a customer review' some way down on the left-hand side, underneath the bar chart.

Goodreads is another place for reviews (just copy and paste your Amazon review), and if you are in the US, you can also leave one on BookBub.

Other ways to help are to tell a friend, post how much you enjoyed the book on social media, recommend *Walking in the Rain* to your book club, ask your local library to get it in.

Thank you so much for your support! Oh, and if you haven't read *Keepers*, you can find that on Amazon too, both paperback and eBook.

Cheryl, February 2023

About the author

When Cheryl Burman moved to the Forest of Dean in SW England she, like Tolkien and Rowling, was inspired to write.

She started with middle grade fantasy, discovered a taste for historical fiction, also that short stories and flash can be fun, and then moved on to historical fantasy. She likes a challenge and a change.

Many of her shorter pieces have been short- and long-listed or awarded prizes and appear in several anthologies.

As Cheryl Mayo, she is Chair of Dean Writers Circle and a founder of Dean Scribblers, which encourages the creative writing spark in young people in the community.

All her books, including purchase links, can be found on her website .

You can also sign up there for *By the Letter*, Cheryl's monthly newsletter, and receive your free eBook as a thank you gift.

Acknowledgements

Many thanks to my critique partners, Jodi and Paula, for living with this book for many months and reading it more than once. Couldn't do this without you. Also thank you to those members of Dean Writers Circle who gave constructive help, especially as beta readers. And to Jo, Mary and Victoria for their beta feedback also.

Finally, my loving thanks to my patient, tolerant husband, David Harris, without whom this book would not exist.

Any spelling, grammatical or design flaws are entirely my own.

Printed by Amazon Italia Logistica S.r.l.
Torrazza Piemonte (TO), Italy